Declan Gates Never Did Know How To Play Nice.

His gaze drifted over the sun-glazed stone of the house, so different from the menacing blackened visage he remembered from his childhood.

The power of the place still moved him. The dark ocean sprawled beneath the wide gray sky; the high granite cliffs; the wheeling, crying seagulls. The sharp, salt tang of the air scratched at a raw place inside him.

He hadn't been here for…what, ten years?

He heard Lily's car engine as she pulled down the drive. *She'd* brought him back.

She always did have that kind of power over him.

Blackrock High's most likely to succeed, Lily Wharton was used to getting what she wanted.

Once, long ago, he'd have given her anything.

But this time lovely Lily Wharton wouldn't get her way.

Dear Reader,

People often ask me: "What's your book about?"

With this story I found myself saying: "It's kind of *Romeo and Juliet* meets *Wuthering Heights* at the stock market… but nobody dies in the end!"

I guess it's obvious that my book isn't *exactly* like those two timeless classics, but hey, I've got star-crossed lovers from feuding families, a craggy, windswept landscape and a brooding hero, haven't I?

Very different ending, though, I'm happy to say.

When a magical romance's story sucks me in, then suddenly one or both of the lovers dies tragically, some people call it moving or satisfying but mostly I call it annoying as heck! I've always felt free to mentally rewrite the endings of books or movies that didn't go where I hoped they would, and I suspect this tendency is one of the many things that turned me into a writer. I love knowing that no matter how much I torment my characters on the way to their happy ending, they will get there.

I hope you enjoy Lily and Declan's story!

Jennifer Lewis

JENNIFER LEWIS

BLACK SHEEP BILLIONAIRE

Published by Silhouette Books
America's Publisher of Contemporary Romance

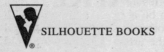

SILHOUETTE BOOKS

ISBN-13: 978-0-373-76847-9
ISBN-10:   0-373-76847-8

BLACK SHEEP BILLIONAIRE

Copyright © 2008 by Jennifer Lewis

All rights reserved. Except for use in any review, the reproduction
or utilization of this work in whole or in part in any form by any
electronic, mechanical or other means, now known or hereafter
invented, including xerography, photocopying and recording, or in
any information storage or retrieval system, is forbidden without
the written permission of the editorial office, Silhouette Books,
233 Broadway, New York, NY 10279 U.S.A.

This is a work of fiction. Names, characters, places and incidents are
either the product of the author's imagination or are used fictitiously, and
any resemblance to actual persons, living or dead, business establishments,
events or locales is entirely coincidental.

This edition published by arrangement with Harlequin Books S.A.

® and TM are trademarks of Harlequin Books S.A., used under license.
Trademarks indicated with ® are registered in the United States Patent
and Trademark Office, the Canadian Trade Marks Office and in other
countries.

Visit Silhouette Books at www.eHarlequin.com

Printed in U.S.A.

Books by Jennifer Lewis

Silhouette Desire

The Boss's Demand #1812
Seduced for the Inheritance #1830
Black Sheep Billionaire #1847

JENNIFER LEWIS

has been dreaming up stories for as long as she can
remember and is thrilled to be able to share them with
readers. She has lived on both sides of the Atlantic, and
she worked in media and the arts before growing bold
enough to put pen to paper. Jennifer is happily settled in
New York with her family, and she would love to hear
from readers at jen@jen-lewis.com.

For LBC, also known as Lynn's Book Chat,
and its fabulous members Abbey, Donna, Kitty
and the eponymous Lynn. I hope we all enjoy
chatting about books for another ten years!

Acknowledgments:

Many thanks to the wonderful people who read this book
while I was writing it, including Amanda, Anne, Carol,
Cynthia, Leeanne, Marie, my agent, Andrea, and my
editor, Demetria. I owe extra gratitude to Amanda
and Carol for their financial expertise.

One

"Have you gone mad?" A deep male voice rang off the high stone walls of the old house.

Lily Wharton whipped her head around.

Recognition flashed through her, hot and sharp, at the sight of that hard, handsome face. *Declan Gates.*

She fought a mad urge to laugh. She might have known Declan would skip over all pleasantries and cut right to the point.

"I'm pruning the roses. As you can see, they're a little overgrown." She gestured at the head-high tangle of thorns around them. She'd been so immersed in trying to tame the old rose garden that she hadn't even heard his car.

"That doesn't explain what you're doing *here,* on the

grounds of *my* house." His aggressive gaze made her skin prickle.

His strong jaw, proud nose and high cheekbones had changed little in ten years, but this new Declan wore a tailored suit, his jet hair slicked back. His broad shoulders and solid chest hinted at hard muscle beneath his fine clothing.

Fierce excitement swelled in her chest. *He'd come back.* "I've been trying to contact you for months. I was sorry to hear about your mother's death."

One black brow lifted.

Lily colored slightly at the knowledge that he'd caught her in a lie. The town of Blackrock, Maine, had heaved a collective sigh of relief when the witch on the hill had finally passed.

"I don't know how many messages I left for you. Your office told me you were in Asia, but you didn't return my calls. I couldn't bear to see the house left empty and forgotten."

"Ah, yes. I'd almost forgotten that it was *your* family's ancestral home."

His pale eyes shimmered in the sun, sparking a trail of memories. She'd fought so hard not to fall under his spell all those years ago, when the unspoken hatred between their families made even friendship a crime.

Even now a familiar sting of attraction made her skin feel tight.

All her plans and the very future of Blackrock rested on this man's goodwill. She was counting on his natural sense of honor and his deep instinct for right and wrong.

But Declan Gates had never been nice.

Heat crept up her neck as she recalled the once-familiar growl of his motorcycle engine. The sound had roared over the town and echoed off the cliffs, making the townspeople gnash their teeth and curse him and his family.

He hadn't cared.

He wasn't bothered by anything so conventional as propriety or other people's feelings.

The last time she'd seen him—ten years ago—he'd thundered right up her driveway and banged on the door. She'd tried to get rid of him fast, before her mother came home. Before he noticed he still made her pulse quicken, and stirred panic mingled with longing in her heart. He'd said he was leaving Blackrock. That he'd *never* come back. And for ten years he'd been as good as his word.

But now she needed him.

His eyes drifted over the front of her striped oxford shirt, along the length of her grubby khakis. Unwelcome heat gathered under his predatory gaze.

"You haven't changed a bit, Lily."

The way he said it, she wasn't sure if it was intended as a compliment or an insult.

"You haven't, either." She swallowed.

"That's where you're wrong."

She tightened her grip on the pruning shears as his words sank in. Ten years was a long time.

One thing hadn't changed. His eyes still seemed to see right through her. To strip her bare of pretensions with their stark intensity.

She inhaled sharply. "This house was chiseled out of the rock more than two hundred years ago with nothing but primitive tools and sweat. Since it's high on a cliff you can see it from everywhere. It's the face of the town. It's not right that it should be left to fall into a ruin."

He stared up at the wide stone walls. "This house used to be black. How did you get it clean?" His voice rang with genuine curiosity.

"I power-washed it. It scoured off all the soot the coal-fired boiler at the mill belched out for decades."

He turned to her. "You felt it was your duty to blast away the sins of the past?"

"I would have asked permission if you'd returned my calls. Blackrock is falling apart, Declan. I hoped that if I cleaned the house it would show people that we can make a fresh start."

She hesitated for a second, then screwed up her courage and took a deep breath. "I want to restore the house and live in it, and I'd like to buy the old mill, too."

Darkness flickered in his eyes. "They're not for sale."

"Why?" Alarm stirred in her heart. "There's nothing for you in Blackrock anymore. The old Gates mill has been closed for a decade, you have no family there, you're successful and have your own life—"

Declan laughed. "What do you know about my life?"

She blinked, unable to respond. She truly didn't know this cool stranger who bore so little resemblance to the rough-edged but caring Declan she remembered.

"Now that my mother is dead, you want to reinstall the ancient and genteel Wharton family in their ancestral home, so they can once again take up their rightful place as Blackrock's first family?"

His accusation tightened her shoulders, but she wasn't going to let past grudges ruin the future of Blackrock. "I have my own company now, creating fabrics and wallpapers. The mill is the perfect place to make my handmade, organic textiles. I want to provide work for the people of Blackrock."

"I'm afraid that won't be possible."

"Why? What do you mean to do with them?" Her chest heaved as she stared at him.

"That's my business." His chiseled features showed no emotion.

Fury mingled with exasperation at his casual dismissal of all her hopes and dreams. "Your business? From what I've read, you're a corporate raider, a vulture capitalist, you buy things so you can tear them apart. Is that your plan for the house and Blackrock?"

He raised a dark brow. "I see you've done your research about me, so I'm sure you know the house is mine to do with what I like. My family bought it from yours."

"They swindled them out of it." She'd heard the story from her cradle. "After my great-grandfather got wiped out in the crash of twenty-nine and committed suicide, his widow was desperate."

"And I'm sure she appreciated the good money she was paid for the old pile."

"Money your family earned on the black market, selling guns and bootleg liquor."

Declan didn't look the least bit rattled. "And rattraps.

My great-grandpa wasn't called Rattrap Gates for nothing. He used to travel the country selling them before we settled here in Blackrock." His eyes gleamed with humor.

"We Gateses may not have been born with silver spoons in our mouths, but we do know how to make a buck, and when it comes right down to it, that's what counts." He crossed his expensively suited arms over his broad chest.

"No, it isn't. People count. Happiness is what matters." Heat surged in her chest.

"Oh, really." His grim smile unnerved her. "So why do you need the house back to be happy?"

"Because it's a beautiful old house that deserves to be treasured."

"How would you know? You never came inside it, not when we were kids."

She shrank a little. He was right.

"You never invited me." Her protest sounded false. They both knew she never would have come even if he had. Her mother would have gone berserk if she even had any idea they were friends.

"Have you been inside now?" His narrowed eyes amounted to an accusation.

"No," she answered honestly. "The door's locked and I don't have the key."

He laughed. "You always were a straight shooter, Lily." Then his expression hardened. "Up to a point."

"I love this town, Declan. I've spent most of my life here, and I'd like to spend the rest of it here, too. But Blackrock is under siege right now. There's been no work here for ten years since your mother closed the pulp mill—"

Declan held up his hand. "Wait a second, are you telling me you're sorry my mother closed the mill? I remember you leading a protest, shouting about air pollution and poisoned water and how the mill was ruining the quality of life in the town. You were quite the crusader with your billboards and your smug friends." His ice-colored eyes glittered.

She swallowed. "I deserved that. It must have hurt to have people up in arms about the factory your family owned."

Declan chuckled. A cold, metallic sound so different from the raw passionate laughter she remembered. "I remember one sign that said the sulfurous emissions from our mill made the town smell like Hell, and it had a picture of me as the devil." He paused and pinned her with his gaze. "I've been doing my best to live up to that one ever since."

Heat rose to her cheeks. She didn't recall the sign, but she'd been young and callous. Full of ideals and energy.

She cleared her throat. "I've learned a lot since then. Clean air and water don't mean so much if you can't earn money to eat."

"And now Good Queen Lily's going to save the town?"

"It would be a win-win situation. I get to live and run my business from the town I love, and my wallpaper factory will bring work to the town."

"A wallpaper factory hardly uses the same skills and equipment as a pulp mill."

"I'll retrain the workers. I plan to keep the old brick building's shell but entirely refit it. I'll certainly get rid of the coal-fired boiler that turned this town black."

"Shame." His eyes glinted. "A coating of soot fits the town so nicely. It won't be familiar old Blackrock anymore if it all looks like *this*." He gestured at the back of the house, which faced the rose garden.

Soft afternoon sun bathed the sparkling stone in warm light. Windows caked with grime for decades now shone like bright eyes. Three stories high, the house was a fine example of classically inspired Georgian architecture. Simple and unpretentious, it perfectly suited its rugged and demanding environment.

A thrill rushed through her at the sight of it restored to its former glory. "Doesn't it look beautiful? The whole town came out to help."

Her chest expanded as she remembered that amazing day. When people looked up over the town and saw what she was doing, men who hadn't worked in years shoved each other aside to relieve her at the power-washer. Women brought sandwiches and lemonade, and by the end of the afternoon there'd been a party of sorts taking place on the weedy terrace, with burgers grilling and people toasting the future of the town with cold beers.

She'd warned them they were trespassing and that her actions were possibly a crime, but they'd all been willing to take the risk.

That afternoon they'd shared a vision. Believed in a new future for Blackrock. "You should have seen it,

Declan. It meant so much to them to see the old house brought back to life."

"You mean to scrub away every trace of the Gates family you all hate so much." His voice sounded calm, but she saw something odd in his expression. A twinge of pain.

A curl of guilt unwound inside her. Guilt at how she'd betrayed their friendship.

Betrayed him.

He straightened his shoulders. "You want this house back so badly, but you're forgetting about the curse that runs with it. All those stories the townspeople tell about it? They're true."

"Oh, rubbish." She fought a frisson of fear. The house still looked somewhat spooky and forbidding through the snarl of briars. It was easy to imagine a sleeping princess and a black-bearded pirate—or worse— hovering in one of the cavernous rooms.

She cleared her throat. "I don't believe in any silly superstitions, but even if the curse does exist it's on your family, not the house."

"Ah, yes. The old curse that makes the Gates men turn bad."

"As if they ever needed any help." Her quip died on her lips as his jaw stiffened. She swallowed hard. "I'm sorry about what happened to your brothers."

She shivered, suddenly cold. The sea air could turn on you like that. She didn't know what exactly had happened to Declan's brothers, but they were gone. Dead before they'd even reached twenty-five.

"Yes." He stared out at the sea, his achingly perfect profile silhouetted against the bright, clear sky. His devilish good looks only enhanced his dangerous reputation as a teen and the years had done nothing to diminish them. If anything he was more agonizingly handsome than ever.

He rubbed a hand over his mouth. "Don't forget my dad. Killed in a mysterious hunting accident." He fixed his ice-gray gaze on her. "I guess I'm the black sheep of the family because I'm beating the odds just by standing here. I'm a survivor."

Determination showed in the set of his jaw. "You won't get rid of me. No one can, not even lovely Lily Wharton."

Lovely Lily. The name he used to call her shot through her with a stab of longing.

My lovely Lily of the fields.

That's where they'd been together. Alone, high on the cliff top, lying in the soft fields of clover, staring up at the clouds. Or running through the mossy woods, laughing, chasing each other. Splashing through a brook hunting for frogs or blowing dandelion clocks until their lungs hurt.

She bit the inside of her mouth as a strange mess of emotions welled near the surface.

They'd been so close.

You're everything to me, Lily. He'd said it to her time and time again. Such a serious look on his face for a boy so young. What had they been, fourteen? Fifteen?

She gulped and grabbed for her gardening gloves where they lay among the thorns. A long barb scratched her arm and left a trail of white ending in a speck of blood.

"Are you hurt?" Declan's brow creased. He reached out to her but she jumped back as if he might bite her.

His expression flattened. "Still afraid of me, huh?"

She swallowed, clutching her scratched wrist.

"Or afraid of your own feelings for me? Feelings too dark and primal for a Wharton?" His eyes narrowed. She resisted the urge to step backward into the barbed thickets.

Long ago Declan had found and tapped a wild streak deep inside her. He'd turned their youth into an adventure that still lived in her most treasured memories.

He'd always seemed to feel more deeply than other people and to live life with greater intensity. Declan had always been up for something new—tracking coyotes in the woods, swimming in forbidden surf, scrambling over rocks and unleashing dreams that threatened to fly too close to the sun in their wild ambition.

But childhood didn't last forever.

"This what you were afraid of, Lily?" He nodded at the forbidding tangle of thorns that covered the walled garden. "Afraid that if you didn't prune your emotions and nip your desires in the bud, they'd end up running rampant, out of control?"

She held her tongue as her thoughts threatened to tread long-forbidden paths.

"These highly bred tea roses do need a lot of pruning." He braved the thorns to grab a thick, woody stem between two strong fingertips. "If they're not tended they grow into an ugly snarl and don't flower."

He pulled back his hand. "Wild roses are different. They thrive in conditions that would kill most other plants. They don't mind the wind or the cold or the salt air. They just hang in there and grow whether anyone cares about them or not."

He stepped toward her. Crowded her. The male scent of him carried to her on the sea air, the wool of his suit mingled with something darker, more wild.

He tilted his head and looked into her eyes. "Maybe you're a wild rose, Lily. Perhaps you'd grow better if you didn't prune back your emotions so hard."

He lifted his hand and held it out to her like an offering. A challenge.

* * *

Declan didn't really think she'd take his hand, but a strange, raw sensation—something like hope—flashed inside him as she lowered those wide, piercing eyes and grazed his extended palm with her gaze.

A long time had passed since she'd turned up her pert little nose at him. She'd been a child then, under her parents' thumb. Now she was a woman, and a strong, intriguing one.

She still had the same roses and cream complexion, the delicate aristocratic features, the clear aggressive gaze that seemed so warm and yet—

Her eyes snapped back to his face. "I'll thank you to keep your opinions to yourself, Declan Gates. I hardly see that my emotions are any of your business." Two bright spots of color shone high on her smooth cheeks.

Her curt words stung, but with practiced ease he showed no emotion as he drew his hand back. "No. I don't suppose they are. And I'll thank you to leave *my* property alone."

It was easy to be cool when any emotions you'd once endured had been crushed out of you by the people you'd loved.

Including the prim ice princess standing before him.

She swallowed and tucked a loose strand of hair behind her ear. He didn't feel any remorse at seeing her squirm.

He'd learned of her repeated calls to his business numbers, but he knew she didn't want to see *him*. She needed something she could only get from him.

Her hazel eyes sparkled with determination. "I can pay you a fair price for the property. My business is doing well."

Of course. He knew all about Home Designs, Lily's upscale collection of fine textiles and wallpapers to beautify one's life. Lily always was good at papering over things.

He held her gaze. "The house is not for sale, nor is the mill."

She blinked, and for once words didn't flow smoothly off that pretty tongue.

"No glib comebacks? No tactful put-downs? Of course, your old M.O. was to act offended and stalk off like *I* was the one in the wrong."

She glanced around, no doubt embarrassed by his open hostility.

He never took his eyes off her. "Worried someone

will see? I don't care who hears me. You know me, Lily. I never cared what other people thought. That was *your* problem."

A flush rose to her cheeks. "Declan, that's not fair."

"What isn't fair? That I'm accusing you of guarding your reputation at all costs? Or that I won't play nice and give you what you want?"

He hated the desire that grew inside him as he stared into her hazel eyes. With her blond hair and fair complexion, surely her eyes should be cold ice-blue? Instead, as always, they shone like warm honey.

Dangerously seductive.

She lifted her chin. "Think of the people of Blackrock." She twisted her hands together. "The town would come back to life, Declan."

He hesitated, chagrined to notice that her passion for what she believed in still affected him. Lily had always been a fighter, ready to defend the helpless or battle injustice, without regard for who stood in the way.

Lovely Lily, so pure and sweet and kind to everyone—*except him.*

"Blackrock and the Whartons, intertwined as two lovers, a fairy kingdom on the coast of Maine with its own gentle monarchy. Until the Gates family came along and ruined everything." He narrowed his eyes. "Well, you won't be rid of us so easily. I'm keeping the house and the mill."

"And what are you going to do with them?" Her gaze tore into him.

He stared into the face he'd once loved with every

ounce of passion in his soul. "I'm going to let them fall down and crumble into the sea, along with all the ugly memories I have of this hateful place."

Lily stared at him for a moment, speechless. Then she turned and stormed off.

Just like he knew she would.

He stared after her as she strode across the slate terrace and down the stairs to the drive.

He never did know how to play nice.

His gaze drifted over the sun-glazed stone of the house, so different to the menacing blackened visage he remembered from his childhood.

The power of the place still moved him. The dark ocean sprawled beneath the wide gray sky, the high granite cliffs, the wheeling, crying seagulls. The sharp, salt tang of the air scratched at a raw place inside him.

Jesus, he hadn't been here for—what, ten years?

He heard Lily's car engine as she pulled down the drive. *She'd* brought him back.

She always did have that kind of power over him.

He'd been alerted to Lily's little campaign of improvements when a local real estate agent called to see if he wanted to list the house on the market.

Blackrock High's "most likely to succeed," Lily Wharton was used to getting what she wanted.

Once, long ago, he'd have given her anything. But this time lovely Lily Wharton wouldn't get her way.

Two

Lily marched along the Manhattan sidewalk, her heels beating time on the concrete. If money was the only thing that mattered to Declan Gates, then she'd win him over with money. He was a business man and he wouldn't say no to an irresistible proposition.

She was a practical woman. She wouldn't allow a family feud or any personal water under the bridge between her and Declan to ruin the future of Blackrock.

Unable to get an appointment, she'd resorted to trickery to get her face-to-face confrontation.

Pretending to be a driver confused by poor directions, she phoned his offices to ask where to pick him up. She paused in front of the large, midseventies town house and glanced at her handwritten note.

This was it.

With its carved limestone front and gleaming black wrought iron gates, the elegant old house looked like the embassy of a wealthy country. Anxiety tightened her gut. Hopefully she wouldn't be interrupting Declan in negotiations with a foreign premier.

She rang the bell and jumped when it opened almost immediately.

An actual butler, complete with gray-and-black striped pants.

She cleared her throat. "Declan Gates asked me to meet him here." Amazingly easy to lie when you wanted something so badly.

"Come in, madam."

She followed Jeeves across the glistening black-and-white marble foyer to an ornately scrolled antique brass elevator. The butler pressed the button for her before exiting, then the doors slid closed and carried her soundlessly to the third floor.

A harsh, metallic clash startled her as the doors opened into a spacious sunlit room. She blinked at the sight of two men wielding flashing blades. Larger, heavier weapons than the usual skinny fencing foil.

Sharp steel spun through the air, crashed and flew apart. Protective masks concealed the men's identities as they danced around each other with an intriguing blend of elegance and force. Chivalry and brutality.

Unnoticed, Lily watched them for several minutes, thrusting, defending, gaining ground. One had what looked to be perfect form, smooth and stylish, light on his feet.

But the other was more aggressive.

"Gotcha!"

"Damn you, Gates. And you're supposed to say *touché*."

"Whatever. I still got you. And that's the fifteenth time now."

"Your technique needs work but you're a ruthless bastard, I'll give you that."

"I take pride in it."

The man on the left pulled off his helmet, revealing tousled dark hair and flashing pale eyes.

Then he saw her.

Declan held steady as his heart, already pounding with exertion, took another hard kick.

Lily Wharton stood in the scrolled archway at the entrance to the room, lazy afternoon sun making a halo in her loose golden hair. She looked every inch an angel come down to earth.

But he knew different.

He fixed her with a cool stare. "Why, it's lovely Lily Wharton. To what do I owe this pleasure?"

"You're hard to pin down, Declan." Her clipped tones bounced off the polished oak floor.

The color on her cheeks belied her cool demeanor.

He tucked his helmet under his arm and studied her for a moment. Polished and perfect in a crisp gray suit. Tiny pearls shone in her delicate ears, and a thin strand of them ornamented her slim throat.

"Much as it pains me, I suspect you didn't come here to admire my fencing form. Have you met Sir Charles?" He gestured to his opponent, who'd just removed his helmet.

The sandy-haired Brit shook Lily's hand and said he was delighted to meet her.

Irritation prickled in Declan as she uttered a meaningless platitude and anointed Sir Charles with one of her pearly smiles.

"I'm glad Declan didn't run you through." She laughed.

"Not for lack of trying, I'm afraid. I'd watch out for this one if I were you." Sir Charles chuckled at his own joke.

Declan kept his eyes fixed on Lily. "Don't worry, she already knows to be *en garde*. Lily and I go all the way back." Tempered steel shimmered in his voice.

There was a pleasantly awkward pause.

"Well, I'm off to change. See you next week, Declan." Charles headed for the elevator. Declan murmured his assent but didn't take his eyes off Lily.

After the elevator doors closed, she ran a hand through her hair as if to shake him out of it. "Why do you stare at me like that?"

"I went years without seeing you. Just catching up."

Her hair was slightly windblown. It would probably feel soft, like milkweed silk, under his palms.

Flinching from his hard gaze, she turned and strode toward the broad window, her heels clicking on the wood floor. Her suit hugged her trim, feminine form and showcased those long, shapely legs that could haunt a man's dreams for a lifetime.

He looped his steel épée in the air just as she turned to face him. The bright metal flashed in the sun, capturing her in its illusory circle.

She frowned. "Declan, I have a proposition for you."

He lowered his blade. "Sounds intriguing. Dare I hope it involves moonlight on your bare skin?"

She made a little moue of exasperation that only stirred his blood. "I'd like you to name your price for the house."

"I told you, it's not for sale."

"You're a businessman and I'm a businesswoman. We both know that everything has a price. Obviously, in this situation, you hold all the cards so it's a seller's market. But if you name your price…" She lifted her chin. "I'll meet it."

She pursed those prim pink lips and fixed him with her bright gaze.

He fought the urge to laugh. Lily was making the mistake all his opponents made sooner or later. They thought he was all about the money.

He flipped up the blade of his sword and examined the sharp, uncapped point.

For him it was *never* about the money. What turned him on was the game. The chase, the takedown.

The kill.

He pressed his bare finger to the point. Not sharp enough to draw blood.

Unlike his vivid imagination.

"Perhaps I'm the only man you've ever met who doesn't have a price." He let his gaze drift over her sleek body. Sweating inside his fencing gear, he could easily imagine the intense heat he'd feel if he could strip off that tidy suit and run his fingers over her silky skin.

Maybe her mistake was trying to bargain with mere money.

Lily straightened her shoulders inside her tailored suit. "I'll give you five million dollars for the house and the mill."

"Five million?" He blew out a breath and fought the urge to laugh. The real estate agents circling over Black-rock like turkey vultures since his mother's death had told him the combined properties were worth about two and a half million in their current state.

"You'll do anything to be rid of me, won't you, Lily?" He closed his fingers around the handle and pressed his fist to his heart. "That hurts."

Her bright hazel eyes narrowed. "I don't believe anything could hurt you, Declan Gates. You've got about as much feeling as that sword in your hand."

He turned the épée, admiring its polished perfection. He prided himself on being hard and cold, handling his business without emotion.

So why did a fever rise in his blood at the prospect of Lily Wharton trying to buy him out?

As a businessman he should take her offer and laugh all the way to the bank.

But as a *man*…

The sword burned against his palm. "Five million dollars is a lot of money." He cocked his head.

She licked her lips, sending a bolt of raw lust shiver-

ing through him. "I know it's not much to you, Declan.
I know you're worth…billions, but if you sell to me for
five million you'll always know you were compensated
more than fairly."

Fair? Nothing about life was fair. It wasn't fair that
his kindhearted father died of a slow-bleeding gunshot
wound, alone in the woods, leaving his sons with their
cold, unloving mother. It wasn't fair that his wild older
brothers burned too hot and flared out too soon.

It wasn't fair that his lovely Lily had pushed him
away, shunned him and crushed his young heart to a
bloody pulp under her neat tennis shoes.

And as long as he owned those properties Lily
Wharton wanted so badly, he had a controlling stake
in *her* heart.

"Ten million." He held her gaze while he twirled the
épée in his hand. Sharp metal caught the light.

Her eyes widened. She walked toward him, her
elegant body held tightly inside her crisp suit. "Declan,
are you serious?"

"I'm always deadly serious."

She hesitated, thoughtful. "All right."

A stab of pain rang through him at the realization that
she was willing to pay ten million dollars to be done
with him forever.

But he never betrayed emotion. Rarely even felt it
anymore. He tucked his sword under his arm and made
a graceful bow. Then he took her hand.

He raised her fingers to his mouth and kissed them.

Desire rippled through him at the sensation of her

soft fragrant skin pressed against his lips. As he released her hand, he saw a strange look in her eyes. A look that revealed, just for a split second, that she wasn't just a businesswoman—she was a woman.

Her company was small and the profits were no doubt still being reinvested to encourage growth. To raise ten million dollars she'd either have to borrow heavily or take her company public.

Either strategy left her vulnerable to someone who wanted to own her.

This time she wouldn't brush him off so easily.

He'd raise his stake in her heart.

He executed a short bow. "I'll await your capital."

As he backed away, like a medieval courtier too noble to turn his back on the queen, he could almost taste the bittersweet thrill of victory. If he played the hand she'd dealt him, he could have the woman, her company and the house.

"Those money-grubbing Gateses don't give a hang for anything except filthy lucre." Lily's mom stacked the emptied Dresden teacups on a tray. "All that wealth and not one of them ever had an ounce of culture or breeding." She carried the tray into the cramped kitchen of the tiny clapboard colonial that served as the Wharton family home since 1930.

Lily picked up a plate with two scones left on it. "But, Mom, you can't look down your nose at them completely. Their money allowed them to buy our house in the first place. It's only because I've become the first money-grubbing Wharton in recorded history that we have a shot at buying it back."

She followed her mom into the kitchen and stored the scones in the hand-carved bread bin.

"You know I admire your achievements, Lily, and your designs are beautiful, but I can't help thinking you spend altogether too much time on the business side of things. Surely you could hire that out?"

Her mother donned her familiar pink rubber gloves that kept her hands lady-soft even after decades of washing her own dishes.

Lily sighed and slammed the bread bin shut. "I enjoy business, Mom. That's why I went into it. If I didn't have a knack for design, I would have created and marketed something else, like, say, rattraps." She crossed her arms over her chest.

Predictably, her mother didn't look up from the suds in the sink. "Very funny. I know you find me old fashioned but I believe in maintaining a certain standard. The Whartons have always prided themselves on their academic accomplishments, particularly in the area of classical scholarship. With your brain you could have—"

"Mom, get over it. I don't want to be a professor. You know I think Dad was the most wonderful man ever, but I'm not him. I love negotiating and planning and growing my company."

"Well, I just don't think it's very ladylike," muttered her mom, scrubbing suds over a bone-china cup.

Another peaceful afternoon in the country. She couldn't wait to have her own house in Blackrock.

She took a deep breath. "I've decided to take my company public."

"What? You mean, do an IPO?" She pronounced the letters as if they spelled the name of a deadly disease.

"Exactly. With an initial public offering I can raise the money to buy the house and the mill."

"I thought you offered to buy him out and he turned you down." Her mom picked up a printed dishtowel and started to dry a cup.

"I met with him again." She tried to keep her voice casual. She'd had a strange tangled feeling in her stomach ever since. Probably at the prospect of raising, then parting with, ten million dollars.

"You should stay away from him. That boy was always trouble." She peered over the rims of her glasses and fixed Lily with a steel-blue gaze.

Lily resisted the urge to roll her eyes. "I'm not asking him out on a date, Mom. I'm trying to buy back our family home."

"And what did he say?"

"He said he'd sell the house and the mill for ten million dollars."

"Ten million? That's daylight robbery!"

"It's a lot. More than they're worth."

"By a long way, I'll bet."

Lily swallowed. "Yes. But to me they're priceless. With no place for people to work, the town will die out. Blackrock's on its way to becoming a ghost town, Mom. It's never been safe for fishing because of the rocks, and with the mill gone, it has no economic base. Most of the people I went to high school with have moved to Bangor or Portland or out of state. There are so few children being born here that the school will be forced to close in a few years."

She inhaled deeply, trying not to let emotion creep into her voice. "Ten million dollars will be money well spent if it can open a new chapter in the town's future. And it's worth almost as much to get back that beautiful house. It'll last a thousand years if it's cared for. If it's left abandoned the roof will fall in and it'll be a ruin in a few years."

Her mother paused but didn't turn around and didn't say anything. Normally she argued for the sensible approach, but Lily knew how much she wanted that house back in the Wharton family.

"I think you might be right, dear." She pulled the plug in the sink and water gurgled down the drain. "The Gateses have never cared about anything but money, and if that's their language it makes sense to speak it." Her mom slapped her rubber gloves down on the counter. "And once you buy him out, this town will be rid of the Gates family for good."

"Yes." Lily bit her lip.

Maybe you're a wild rose, Lily. Declan's strange statement flashed in her mind and sent a little shiver up her spine.

But he'd just been taunting her, mocking her. He enjoyed putting her on edge, trying to get under her skin. It was a game for him. He didn't care about her any more than she cared about him.

Which was *not at all*.

Three

When the location scout for Macy's department store asked Declan if he'd be willing to rent the Blackrock house out for a catalog shoot, he agreed. Let them hang some curtains and take pictures, at least Lily wouldn't have her hands on the place.

In the weeks since he'd seen her he'd been immersed in a complicated buyout deal involving a Hong Kong manufacturing company that he planned to resell to its rival, so he didn't have time to sweat about Lily Wharton and her scheme to run him out of Maine.

Then his assistant brought the handwritten note on Macy's stationery in with his morning mail.

Declan, the shoot went off without a hitch. The house is a diamond, and no longer in the rough!

Lily's products are so beautiful, you're lucky it costs more to remove them than leave them there. I look forward to working with you again. We have a footwear shoot coming up and I'm already dreaming about your slate patios. Chat soon! Rosemarie.

Declan's fingers tightened around his black lacquered pen. Lily's products?

He dialed the number on the note card, even though by then he'd already figured out the whole scam.

Declan put his new silver BMW Roadster through its paces—and then some—on the road to Blackrock that afternoon and evening. Did nothing hold this woman down? She didn't have the key to get in and redecorate his house by herself, so she'd gone all out and gotten Macy's in on the game?

He gripped the gearshift and steering wheel, wishing sheer speed could cool his blood.

He'd already learned she was taking her company public. The next step in her plan to banish him from Blackrock—and from her sphere of existence—forever.

He honked and sped up as a car moved to cut him off.

She thought it would be so easy to get rid of him, did she? Well, he wasn't a boy anymore and she wasn't going to walk all over him again.

Rosy light bathed the warm stone of the house's impressive facade as he pulled into the driveway, the sun setting behind distant hills. A familiar battered white station wagon sat in the gravel turnaround.

He parked and strode to the front door. "Hello?" His voice rang through the stone-floored entrance hall.

A nasty shiver trickled over him as he realized he hadn't stepped over this threshold in a decade. Last time he'd come up here, to confront Lily, he'd driven away without putting a key in the lock.

The whole place gave him the creeps.

As his eyes adjusted to the gloom, he saw a light shining in a room on the far side of the hall. His mother's old sitting room.

He hesitated, experiencing an unfamiliar apprehension. Was the infamous witch on the hill—to use the more polite version of the phrase—really gone?

Or had she stayed on to haunt the place and make its residents as miserable in death as she'd made them in life?

He walked across the hall, leather soles silent on the dark slate.

A female shriek from the lamp-lit room nearly made him jump out of his suit.

"Oh my God. It's you, Declan. You nearly gave me a heart attack." Lily appeared in the doorway, hand pressed to her heaving chest. Khakis and a ponytail replaced the crisp suit and elegant do of their last encounter. "What are you doing here?"

He stared at her for one incredulous second, then a harsh laugh exploded from his throat. "What am I doing here? It's my damn house. You're not supposed to take possession until *after* I sell it to you."

"I was just tidying up after the shoot. Come in."

She disappeared into the sitting room, beckoning him with her hand.

Speechless, he followed.

Butter-colored paper, sprigged with a subtle pattern of blue-gray leaves, covered the walls. Bulbs shone behind the amber panes of an elaborate arts-and-crafts ceiling fixture that had been broken when he'd lived there.

Thick brocade curtains, with a contrasting pattern of yellow on blue-gray, draped luxuriously across the huge windows. The massive round card table in the center of the room stood liberated from its usual stained green baize and clutter of yellowed newspapers, and glowed with a polished honey sheen.

Inlaid parquet flooring that had always been hidden under an ugly, soiled Victorian rug now gleamed in the warm lamplight.

A paint-blistering curse fell from his lips.

"Declan!" Lily planted her hands on her hips, but her beaming smile revealed her delight at his reaction. "Doesn't the yellow-and-blue contrast bring out the warm tones in all this wood nicely?"

"I can't believe this is the same room." He was too poleaxed to be anything but honest. "I thought the wood was a lot darker than this."

"The finish was caked with grime. Soot from the fireplace most likely, but it polished off really well." She ran a finger over the shiny wooden chair-rail molding that skirted the room. "Chestnut, I think. The craftsmanship is exquisite. The door is carved from a solid slab—isn't that wild?"

The ceiling shone with a fresh coat of white paint, and for the first time he noticed a geometric relief pattern in the plaster.

"It looked even better yesterday, with all the lovely knickknacks and extra pieces of furniture Macy's brought. They took all that stuff back, of course, but it didn't make sense to strip off the wallpaper or remove curtains and slipcovers that were made to fit the furniture already in the house, so they're still here. Look how nicely this chaise longue turned out."

She plunked down on an elegant piece of furniture freshly covered in more of the slate-blue fabric, this time with a copper accent to the pattern.

Declan realized with a fierce jolt that the chaise Lily bounced on so cheerily was his mother's personal throne. He couldn't remember ever seeing it without one of her voluminous dark caftans covering it almost completely. Though mostly he'd tried to stay out of her way.

Was this really the same room? The same house?

"That was my mother's chair."

"Oh my gosh." Lily sprang up, embarrassment heating her face. "I'm sorry. I'm being callous, aren't I? I know you weren't close, but family is family."

Declan's pale eyes scanned the room and he ran a hand through his hair, disordering its shiny black perfection. He looked…stunned.

She'd become so excited by the incredible transformation inside the house that she'd almost forgotten it was Declan's family home. The place he'd grown up.

She bit her lip. He probably felt the way the last Wharton inhabitants did after the Gates family moved in and put their feet up on the Whartons' old treasures.

Being Declan Gates he probably preferred cracked plaster and rattling uncurtained windows to cozy domestic comfort. "You hate it, don't you?"

"No." He frowned. "It looks..." he scanned her gravure printed wallpaper and embroidered textiles "...beautiful."

"Thank you." She managed not to look too astonished. The strange expression on his face unnerved her. His hard mask of unshakeable sangfroid had slipped. She found herself wanting to step forward and touch him. Reassure him somehow.

But she didn't.

"These are from my new mass-market line that'll be available at Macy's, starting next spring. I think we've done a great job creating a handmade look at a machine-made price. I'm glad we were able to take some effective photographs to promote them. I've very excited about these new products."

Declan glanced at her as if he didn't quite understand her. Then his mask slid back into place. "I'm sure the pictures will be most effective. I'd have charged Macy's a higher fee if I'd known you were behind it."

She crossed her arms. "If you'd known I was behind it, you'd have said no."

"True. Though I doubt that would have stopped you." Something glinted in his diamond eyes—a flash of humor? "How much of the house did you renovate? I'm sure you didn't stop at one room."

She licked her lips. Swallowed. "The library, the dining room and two upstairs bedrooms. Just enough rooms to show off the different collections."

He let out one of his bone-rattling laughs. "I'm surprised you haven't changed the locks."

"You *did* give Rosemarie permission to make any nonstructural changes she wanted. She picked the rooms and decided how to decorate them. I just provided the supplies." Had she overstepped the mark? She was so proud of how beautiful the old house looked now.

He looked at her steadily, a sly smile hinting at the corners of his mouth. "I'm sure it was *all* her idea. I'm glad you did the bedrooms. You never know, I might sleep over."

Lily's heart seized. Would he fall in love with the house and refuse to sell it? "You haven't slept here since you left high school."

"You wouldn't want to, either, if you knew the place like I did." He narrowed his eyes and shot her a threatening look.

True, spine-chilling gloom had been her first impression of the house. But now that she'd brightened the rooms and most of the lights worked, it felt quite comfortable. A little big for a normal human habitat, but—

"I bet you haven't been down in the cellar." The menace in his voice sent a chill skittering along her spine.

"No, I—" An involuntary gulp choked off her speech. She cleared her throat. "The door's locked and the key wasn't on that ring you gave Rosemarie. What's down there?"

He shrugged. The movement drew her attention to the way his elegant dark gray suit accommodated his broad shoulders and slim waist. Since he spent his leisure hours trying to intimidate his opponents into submission with a metal blade, she should hardly be surprised he was fit. Who cared? She had no interest in thinking about the hard body beneath his suit.

"Me and my brothers were never allowed down there. *Secrets,* my mom used to say." He cocked his head.

"What kind of secrets?" She tried to show no more than polite interest.

"You know my family wasn't always on the up and up." His mouth tilted into a wry smile. "That we used to trade in black-market guns and ammo."

"And bootleg liquor."

"Yes, the old moonshine. Famous throughout the Northeast. Got everyone in town drunk one time or another, I'd bet."

"When did they stop making it?"

He shrugged again. She ignored the curl of heat low in her belly.

"I guess it stopped being profitable once prohibition ended and cheap legal booze was everywhere. That's when they got the pulp mill going. Turned legit." He gave her a cool smile. "Brought the invigorating smell of sulfur to town." His nostrils flared as if testing the air for brimstone. "I wouldn't go down in that basement if I were you."

"What rubbish. You talk as though there might be skeletons down there." She hid an involuntary shudder.

She wouldn't put anything past Arabella Gates, and the witch on the hill was the only other member of the evil clan she'd actually met. His brothers were older and had dropped out of high school and disappeared by the time she got there, surviving only in local legend.

"Skeletons?" He raised a brow. "Could be. While prohibition lasted, they held a speakeasy here on Friday and Saturday nights. People get drunk and crazy. Fights get started. You know how it is."

She pursed her lips. "I'm happy to say I have no idea how it is. I've never been drunk in my life and I avoid degenerate party animals, thank you." She wouldn't be where she was today if she'd spent her college years out carousing at keg parties instead of sitting hunched over in a library carrel.

He cocked his head and winked. "Shame."

Outrage rippled through her along with a disturbing sensation that almost buckled her knees. She straightened her shoulders, and ignored the unpleasant tightening of her nipples. "You're incorrigible, Declan Gates."

"Yeah." He held her gaze with those ice-cool eyes. "But what you find down there might make you change your mind about paying ten million dollars for the house."

Ten million dollars. The number still made her break out in a sweat. "I don't believe a word of it. I'm going down there right now."

"How are you going to do that without a key?"

Declan shoved his hands in his pockets and leaned against the wall.

"I'll break the door down."

"It's solid wood."

"I'll find a way."

"I don't doubt you will. Have fun."

As it turned out, Declan did most of the work. It took an hour, a screwdriver and a bottle of vegetable oil.

"Watch out, you'll get oil on your nice suit." Lily held her breath as he shoved his whole body weight against the door with a loud thump.

Since the deadbolt lock proved unpickable, they'd unscrewed the heavy wrought iron hinges and poured oil into the almost nonexistent gap between the door and the frame. All that remained was to push the greased door in through the opening and hope the bolt was loose enough to pop out easily. Easier said than done.

"Hand me that ax."

Lily picked up the heavy weapon they'd found in the neglected carriage house, its blade reddened with…rust?

She winced as he bumped the ax handle against the edge of the door, working his way down its length.

"I hope there aren't rats down there," said Declan grimly. "You know, scavenging among the bones."

"Oh, stop it. You know there's probably nothing down there but old junk." She tugged her eyes from the broad muscle of his back straining the seams of his elegant suit.

Once again he shouldered the heavy door. This time it gave and the bolt slid free. He caught himself on the frame with both hands as the door clattered to the stone stairs and wedged itself across them.

"Door's blocking the way," he murmured.

"Never mind. I'll climb over it."

"Knock yourself out. I'll be right here." Declan leaned against the frame. Lily pushed past him, accidentally touching the hot skin of his hand. She ignored the ripple of heat that stung her fingers.

She climbed down the stairs over the fallen door and headed into the darkness. Declan Gates could try his best to scare her off but she wasn't so easily—

"Aeeeeiiiik!" Gleaming rows of spectral shapes shimmered before her in the dark.

"You okay?" Declan's gruff voice rang down the stairs, followed by his footsteps as he clambered over the door after her.

"Yes." She cleared her throat as her cheeks scorched with humiliation. "Fine. Something startled me. Is there a light switch?"

"Hell if I know. I've never been down here." He now stood right beside her, his stirring male scent heated by exertion. Relief surged through her at having a large tough man beside her down in this creepy dungeon.

Then he stepped forward into the darkness.

"Wait for me!" she squeaked. "It *is* kind of spooky."

"What the heck are those things?" His deep voice rang off the stone walls and floor.

She saw Declan's hand reach out to the transparent apparitions that made her squawk like a baby.

"Glass. Big glass bottles." He rapped his knuckles on it. "Got some liquid in it."

"How weird. Hey, is that chain a light switch?" She could just make out a hanging cord near the bottles. Declan reached a long arm up and tugged on it. A florescent strip light hummed and flickered to life, illuminating its collection of dead insects and filling the huge basement with cool pale light.

"Wow. What the heck is this stuff?" Lily stared at rows and rows of dusty bottles.

Declan left her side and paced around the room. The expression on his hard, handsome face was unreadable. He stopped, shook his head and laughed.

It was such a bold laugh, so loud and genuine, that she couldn't help joining in, even though she didn't know what she was laughing at.

Declan ran a hand over one of the big jars. Caressed it like a woman's body with his long fingers. The gesture sent a little shimmer of heat to her belly.

"This is it?" His broad smile almost took her breath away. "I used to think my mom had people strung up down here. That the floor was damp with blood. All this time she was just running the old still to make her favorite tonic."

He shook his head again, then laughed and ran a hand over his face. "Just shows, you think you know people, but you never really do."

So true. Lily stared in amazement at a Declan Gates she hadn't seen before. Well, not for more than ten years. His striking face shone with boyish good humor.

"I guess this is the still." He rapped his knuckles on the sheet metal of what looked like a large water heater. "Look, these jars are freshly made. There's gallons of the stuff down here."

"She must have been brewing until the day she died." Lily scanned the room. "What on earth was she doing with it?"

Declan chuckled. "Drinking it. She always had a bottle of something stashed in her pocket. Called it her nerve tonic. This stuff'll calm your nerves, all right."

He uncapped one of the big bottles and took a whiff. "Damn."

"You never tried it before?"

"Nope. Even the Gates family doesn't serve moonshine to the kids." He shot her a glance but he didn't look bitter, just amused. "Now that you mention it, I'd like to try some. See what all the fuss was about. They say you can drink it all night and not get a hangover."

Lily screwed up her nose. "I bet it tastes terrible."

"Don't knock it. This hooch made my family the money that bought this house." His eyes gleamed in the florescent light.

"You seem to be forgetting that it's *illegal*." She crossed her arms over her chest.

He cocked his head. "Doesn't that seem unfair when you can legally brew your own beer and wine at home?"

"Distilled liquor is different. It's a lot more dangerous. One misstep and you've made deadly poison. And for another thing, it's a major fire hazard. This entire room is a powder keg waiting to blow." The prospect of a lit fuse in her ten million dollar investment itched her like an attack of hives.

His smile faded. "You're right. This stuff is probably two hundred proof. I need to get rid of it." He frowned.

"If you pour it down the drain it might fry the septic system. And if you hire someone to cart it away you could end up with sticky legal hassles." That certainly didn't serve her purposes.

"Yeah." Declan took another sniff from the open bottle. "Damn."

She straightened her shoulders. "I'll help you move it. We'll take it out, pour it over the cliff and hose out the bottles."

"Are you serious?" Declan squinted at her. "Why would you help me do all that?"

"From the goodness of my heart." She smiled primly.

His face cracked into a wicked grin. "Yeah, right. You just want to make sure nothing gets in the way of you kicking my ass out of town and taking up residence on your throne here."

"You're welcome to interpret my motives any way you like, if it gives you pleasure." She rolled up the sleeves of her blouse. "So shall we get started?"

It took both of them to lift one massive, filled bottle. With the door shifted off the stairs, they began the arduous process of hiking each one off the shelf, getting a good grip on it, then walking face-to-face to the stairs, up them and outside.

Inches from each other the whole time.

Touching Declan was unavoidable. Their hands met

on the slippery undersides of the big glass jars, their knees bumped on the stairs, sometimes their arms and shoulders brushed each other.

The warm summer air heated her blood and the exertion made her heart pump. Her elevated temperature and pulse had nothing to do with Declan.

"We could pour it out right here on the patio." Declan shrugged off his suit jacket as they paused for a breather outside. A bright full moon illuminated his white shirt.

She took a deep breath. "I bet it would do a great job of killing the weeds—possibly for the next century—but I think Mother Earth would appreciate us diluting it with a lot of ocean water." She wiped a bead of perspiration off her upper lip. "It pains me to say it, but I think we need to carry them all the way down to the surf. Isn't there a stone staircase somewhere leading down to a beach?"

"The hidden inlet. My brothers and I always called it the pirate cove. That's a lot of stairs. It'll be quite a workout. Are you sure you're up for it?"

"Of course!"

After fifteen bottles she was wiped out. At the bottom of the stairs they plunked the bottle down on the sand and she threw herself down next to it. The salty sea spray felt like heaven on her hot skin. "White flag. I need a break."

Declan hadn't broken a sweat. His shirtsleeves weren't even rolled up, but he sat on the sand next to her without a snide remark. Unscrewed the lid.

Lily gasped for air. "I'll help you pour it out in a sec. I just have to catch my breath first. I'm getting light-headed."

"Speaking of light-headed, I'm going to try the stuff before it's all gone." He whipped a small silver cup out of his pants pocket. She recognized it as part of an eighteenth-century punchbowl set Macy's had found under one of the beds and polished for the shoot. He must have swiped the cup off the dining-room sideboard.

She reminded herself it *was* technically his.

He maneuvered onto his knees and picked up the bottle. Somehow he managed to pick it up all by himself, which he hadn't been able to do before. The clear liquid splashed as he poured a finger or two into the cup.

"May I offer you refreshments?" He held the cup out with an expression of polite inquiry that made her chuckle.

"No, thanks. I enjoy having a stomach lining." She certainly could use a drink after all the exertion, but homemade hooch was *not* what the doctor ordered.

"Drinking moonshine in the moonshine." Declan held the cup up and it shone in the bright moonlight. "Kind of poetic."

He took a sip. His eyes narrowed and his brow furrowed. Then he nodded. He drained the cup. "It's good. Smooth. Sort of sweet."

Waves lapped the rocks that surrounded the tiny beach, and the sound of water enhanced a sudden punishing thirst.

Declan poured more glistening liquid into the pretty silver punch cup. He swirled it and peered into its crystal depths. "I'm feeling all warm inside." He shot her a mellow smile.

The moon glazed his features and picked out the

sharp cut of his cheekbones, that determined jaw. She watched his Adam's apple as he sipped again.

He looked up. "I can see why they sold a lot of this stuff. It's got no bite to it. Goes down like liquid silk." The night breeze tossed his black hair on his forehead as he held out the cup. "Try it."

"No, really, I don't drink much. I don't think it's a good idea." Her tongue felt like paper in her dry mouth.

"You just don't want to share the cup with me. Afraid you'll catch something." His diamond stare twinkled a challenge. "Makes sense. We were friends up until the time I kissed you. You didn't want your lips on mine, I guess." He drained the cup.

She flinched from his accusation. "You'll get drunk. How will we move those bottles, then?"

"I never get drunk. Was kissing me really that bad?" He tilted his head. For a split second he let a flash of vulnerability show in his eyes. It jolted her heart like a bolt of lightning.

She braced herself. "I don't remember. It was a long time ago." The lie seared her parched tongue.

Oh, she remembered, all right. That kiss had opened up a rift in her life like the San Andreas Fault. All events could be divided into Before and After.

Before, she'd been a bright but ordinary kid whose biggest worry in life was whether she'd ever own a pony. (Answer: no).

After?

The sharp new emotions and thick, unnameable sensations she'd experienced that night shuddered through her heart and soul. By morning they'd heaved up a mountain range of fierce desire snowcapped with pure, ice-cold fear.

Her mother's grim warnings rang in her ears, mingled with whispered gossip about the Gates boys that set the locker rooms abuzz.

She'd avoided him all the next day. And the next. Stayed away from their favorite haunts.

Dodged him on Main Street.

Snubbed him in the school hallway.

Shame soaked into her like salt spray as she remembered how cruelly she'd treated him. Out of her depth, naive, clueless and afraid. Suddenly their innocent—if covert—friendship had changed into something that threatened the neatly woven fabric of her whole existence.

So she'd neatly cut him out of her life.

"I'll never forget that kiss." Declan's husky declaration yanked her back to the present. "One of the highlights of my life."

She shivered, cold despite the warm night air. She'd hacked off a part of herself when she cut Declan out of her life. The wild side of her that craved adventure and excitement. Was it gone for good?

"Go on. Live a little." Declan held out the silver cup, freshly wet with crystal liquid. His silver eyes glinted in the moonlight as his low voice trickled into her ears. "I dare you."

The next thing she knew, she'd seized the cup from his hand and knocked back its contents in one fiery swallow.

Four

The cool liquid slid down Lily's dry throat, sweet and smooth.

"Good, huh?" Declan tilted his head. Moonlight glittered on the dark ocean behind him.

She handed back the cup and wiped her lips with her fingers as delicately as possible.

"Not bad," she managed. Blackrock's famous "white lightning" filtered into her bloodstream, sparking a million pinpoints of light and heat. She caught her breath.

Declan's handsome face shone with a bright, affectionate look that suddenly seemed agonizingly familiar even after more than a decade. His eyelashes hid his eyes for a moment as he splashed more liquid into the silver cup. He held it out, and his piercing gaze rocked her.

"No, thanks." She scrambled to her feet, heart pounding. "We should pour it out."

I dare you.

Declan's words roared in her ears, louder than the surf pounding on the beach, filled with meaning far beyond sipping a forbidden drink.

He climbed to his feet. "The tide's going out. We keep having to walk farther with each trip."

The wind whipped his black hair across his forehead as he held the cup high. "Last taste. To old times." He knocked back the cup and let out a long sigh. "It's rare when something tastes sweeter than you ever imagined."

Like that kiss.

As a teen she'd dreamed about kissing Declan. Sprawled alone on her bed, surrounded by her stuffed animals and posters of pop stars. Pressing her strawberry glossed lips together and wondering.

The reality had been so different than her childish fantasies. The kiss hadn't tasted of strawberries. It was raw and dark, earthy and mysterious and beautiful and frightening.

The sensations that roiled through her hadn't felt soft and reassuring like the embrace of a familiar stuffed toy. They were sharp and hard and fierce, scratching her skin, clawing at her insides, scraping her raw.

"You okay, Lily?" Declan's brow furrowed in the moonlight.

"Of course." She sucked in a breath of salt air. "Let's dump this one." She squatted down to pick up the big jug, and Declan mirrored her motions.

Their fingers brushed each other—soft and hot—a stark contrast with the cool, shiny glass surface. She tugged her eyes from his painfully familiar face and her glance fell to his neck, where his white shirt collar lay unbuttoned to reveal his tan throat.

"They're not getting any lighter, are they?" His Adam's apple moved when he spoke. "We're probably only halfway through."

"We'll get there." She kept her voice level, free of emotion. "One step at a time."

"Determined as ever, aren't you, Lily?"

Something in the tone of his voice made her look up. His eyes were almost black.

"Yes. Yes, I am." She struggled to sound confident.

"I always liked that about you. That you never quit trying. That nothing daunts you."

I wouldn't say that.

That kiss had frightened the hell out of her. Had threatened her self-control and shaken her self-confidence. She'd probably never been quite the same since.

"I'm like you, Lily." He shifted his grip on the bottle. Liquid sloshed and his broad fingertips bumped hers. "I never give up."

"We're nothing alike." She said it too loud, too forceful. Trying to convince herself.

"Why? Because I'm wild and reckless?" His eyes flashed.

The alcohol splashed in the bottle as she hefted it higher.

"I know you like no one else does. Underneath that

veneer of respectability you work so hard to maintain, you're as wild as these cliffs, as the dune grass, as this big black ocean."

Lily blew out a sharp breath somewhere between a laugh and a gasp. His words clanged inside her mind. Her, wild? Maybe a long time ago…

Her shoes sank into the soft, wet sand left by the receding tide, and she struggled to keep her footing.

Suddenly a splashy rogue wave whipped at them, soaking her to the knees.

She shrieked like a girl and dropped the bottle, causing Declan to lose his grip. The jug plummeted into the white foam and a swift riptide pulled it out under the breakers.

For a second she fought the urge to charge after it, then Declan's hands steadied her.

"Come in, the tide's strong." He seized her hand and tugged her back to the bare sand.

"It's floating away." Her chest heaved and loose hair whipped about her face.

"And we never even put a message in it." Declan's deep voice rang with humor.

He turned to look at her. "You're shaking." His tone more serious, he planted his arm around her back and guided her across the sucking wet sand.

His broad hand settled at her waist, pulling the rough cotton of her striped oxford shirt tight over the thin fabric of her bra.

"I'm wet." She tried to distract herself from the strange hot sensation swelling in her chest. Her wet sneakers squelched audibly.

"Me, too. Feels good."

She glanced at him, irked by his careless attitude. "Why are you smiling? Your leather shoes are probably ruined and that soaked wool suit looks pricey."

"It was." His eyes gleamed.

His arm still lay heavy around her waist, and she drew in a breath trying to suck her skin away from his touch. "I suppose you have a closet full of them."

"I do." He shot her a cheery grin.

Suddenly the smile vanished from his face and he stopped walking. Her momentum continued for a half step before his powerful arm stopped her motion.

"What?" She turned, frowning at the way sensation gathered under his fingers.

The harsh moonlight picked out a furrow between his brows and the pale glitter of his eyes. His expression looked confused more than anything else. He raised his free hand and pushed a fluttering strand of hair from her eyes.

"Lily." His soft voice barely rose above the roar of the surf. "My lovely Lily. The woman I always wanted more than anything else in the world."

His words crept through the warm night air and wrapped themselves around her heart. "I wanted you, too, Declan." The words flew out of her mouth and onto the night breeze before she could stop them.

"I know you did. We were made for each other, you and I." One arm still around her waist, he cupped her chin and brushed her lips with his thumb. The sensation sent a shiver of longing dancing over her skin.

"I was young." Her protest of innocence sounded so feeble. "I was afraid."

"I understood. It hurt like hell, but I did understand." He looked at her with honesty and directness that cut to her core.

"You must have hated me." Heat rose over her skin as she remembered her cold, crude rejection.

"I could never hate you."

I love you.

The unspoken words danced between them. She wanted to say them, even though they weren't true and never had been. Somehow saying them would be like salve on an open wound left to fester for ten long years.

But she didn't, because Declan pulled her close and lowered his mouth to hers, depriving her of words and thoughts.

Waves crashed against the rocks as emotion smashed through her. Declan's arms gathered her while their lips parted and they gave their tongues to each other, tasting and exploring.

Her fingertips pressed into his shirt, eager for the warmth of his skin. She moaned softly as Declan licked her lips and rained kisses over her cheeks. She deepened the embrace, pulling him tight with her arms.

The clean raw, male scent of him mingled with the salt spray in the air and tormented her senses to painful arousal.

She rubbed her sensitive fingertips over his cheeks and chin, enjoying their rough, masculine warmth. Her nipples swelled and stung inside her shirt. She pressed herself against his hard chest, writhed against him until the barrier of their clothes became unbearable.

Her fingers tugged at the buttons of his shirt, pulling at the cloth and yanking it away from his skin. She felt his fingers on her shirt, tugging it loose from her pants and roaming inside until his broad hands splayed over the skin of her back.

In an instant he'd unhooked her bra and freed her breasts. The air on her skin made her gasp. She opened her eyes for a split second and was moved to see Declan's eyes firmly closed. A strange expression, dreamlike yet intense, played across his strong features in the moonlight, as if he'd been transported to another dimension.

Her eyes slid shut as she joined him there. She pushed his shirt back over his shoulders and enjoyed the roping muscle of his arms with her fingertips. His chest was deep and thickly muscled, a surprise after the sleek, white surface of his shirt and the slim boyish body she remembered.

A sprinkling of coarse hair was another revelation. This Declan was different from the young boy she knew, just as she wasn't a shy girl anymore.

She was a woman now, and never more painfully aware of it than when Declan settled her onto the cool sand, lifted her shirt and lowered his hot mouth over her breast.

She arched her back and felt the damp sand shift under her as she moaned and writhed at the sensation he roused inside her with his lips, teeth and tongue.

She struggled with his leather belt, finally pulling

it loose from its loops and grappling with the zipper of his pants.

Need built to an agonizing crescendo as she pushed his pants and boxers down over the firm, hard muscle of his athletic backside. Under her the sand felt warm, its slight abrasiveness heightening the intensity of sensation.

Declan's deft fingers undid her shirt and slid her pants and panties down over her legs until she was bare and damp on the bare, damp sand, every inch of her humming with unbearable arousal.

He knelt over her, his hands planted on either side of her shoulders. His hair hung over his forehead and though his eyes were open, that same rapt expression lit his handsome face.

He reached into the pocket of his pants, which lay crumpled on the ground behind him. She didn't dare look at the arousal his clothes no longer hid from view. She kept her eyes instead on the tan skin of his chest with its swirl of black hair, while he ripped open a condom packet and sheathed himself.

His eyes closed again, their soft black lashes a seductive contrast with the masculinity of his features. Her belly shimmered with heat and anticipation as he lowered himself over her.

He shifted his arms alongside hers, his thick forearms running along the length of her upper arms on the sand, his hands cupping her shoulders. The tender possessive gesture tugged at her core and made her crave him deep inside her.

The woman I always wanted more than anything in

the world. She could feel his passion in his touch, hear it in the catch of his breath.

Slick and ready, she lifted her hips and he entered her. She stretched, welcoming him deep inside her, as he filled her. His breath hot on her neck, Declan released a rough, raw sound laden with emotion that tore at her gut.

Relief. That's what it sounded like. Sheer, bone-rattling, drought-quenching relief.

And she felt it, too, ringing right to her toes. The beautiful bittersweet relief of making love to the one man she'd always known, always craved.

Always loved.

She wound her arms around his neck and clutched him close. He began to move his hips, pushing gently into her, rocking her in the spongy sand as he caressed her arms with his fingers and layered soft kisses over her face and mouth.

He was so gentle, his breath soft on her skin, his touch tentative. She could feel him holding back, treating her like something precious, breakable.

The crashing surf echoed the roar of blood in her brain and body as tension built inside her. Declan's fierce passion—held tight and controlled—drove her almost to the brink of madness. She moved her hips, writhing under him, fighting with him, pleading with him to abandon all restraint.

She'd held back her whole life. Kept herself in check, played by the rules.

Been nice.

Now she was ready to let go. Ready to abandon the safe route and jump over the edge of the precipice—

If he would jump with her.

Declan accepted her silent summons. He thrust into her, his breathing erratic, moving at last with a ferocity that mirrored his fiery nature.

He drove her deeper and deeper into a frenzy of excitement that made her want to scream above the roar of the waves.

Sensation ripped through her, blasting her into another dimension like a jet breaking the sound barrier. Her nails dug into Declan's back as she rolled her hips against his, deepening their touch to an impossible, perfect, closeness.

Everything else fell away. All her plans, her dreams, her hard work, her reputation, her fears.

Everything.

Until there was nothing left but her and Declan, hot and sweaty and sandy, moving together and holding each other—so tight—as if they could never let go.

Her climax burst over her like a breaker, shattered her and flung her to the damp sand. At the same instant Declan let go a shout of joy and spasmed inside her.

He collapsed onto her, his chest heavy on hers, as he throbbed inside her quivering body.

"Lily." The rasp of his voice shivered into her ear.

She opened her eyes. His stayed shut tight as he held her in his embrace. A shuddering breath escaped his lips and tangled in her damp hair.

Emotion ripped through her like an undertow as she

realized she'd been waiting her whole life for this moment. Declan had been her closest friend and sole confidant. The person she shared her hopes and dreams with. He was the one person she could always count on to share her joy in something as simple as a steep, treeless track in the woods just wide enough for a sled.

Then he'd opened the door to a powerful new realm of sensation and a world of feelings she'd never dreamed existed.

And she'd slammed that door shut and run in the opposite direction.

But now…

Declan rolled, holding her close to his chest, until she was on top. The warm night air kissed her skin under its sandy layer of tiny crystals. Still inside her, he throbbed once, a deep touch that made her shiver with delight.

"I've missed you." His crystal eyes shone bright in the moonlight. "I've never been so close to anyone."

"Me, neither. I've always felt a special connection with you." The frank admission was the only answer she could give. "And I lied about the kiss. I never forgot it. How could I? It was too, too intense…"

"Too scary." He reached up and brushed a strand of hair behind her ear with sandy fingers. "It scared me, too, that I could feel that much for anyone." The moon glazed the ridges of his face. "And, as it turned out, I was right to be wary." His narrowed eyes glittered.

"We were too young."

"We got older. We were in the same high school for, what, three years after that?"

"I was afraid."

"Afraid of what would happen if you let yourself cross over to the dark side with Dangerous Declan." He cocked his head. His gaze had a feral glitter. "And now you have, how does it feel?"

"Damn good." A laugh exploded in her chest and burst out of her mouth. His chest rocked under hers and they rolled apart as his laughter echoed hers.

"You're all sandy." His fingers grazed the fine grit on her thigh as they lay side by side. He shot a glance at the surf.

Small waves lapped at the shore, the white surf glittering in the moonlight.

"Race you." Before the words were out of her mouth she sprang to her feet and tore across the wet sand to the water.

Her toes tingled and stung as she splashed into the lace collar of frothy water splayed over the sand. She heard Declan's breathing heavy behind her, but gasped with surprise as he flung his arms around her and buried his face in her hair.

"Damn, you're beautiful." He rubbed his face in the tangled mess. "And you smell like heaven."

She arched her back, leaning into him. Shock mingled with excitement that she'd gone streaking across a beach.

Declan pulled her roughly around until they faced each other. He held her at arms length as he drank in the sight of her naked body with hungry eyes.

And she didn't feel a lick of shame.

She never had when she was with Declan. Everything

they did seemed…fun. Right. The way things were supposed to be.

It was always everyone else who was wrong. Her mother. The silly girls in the locker room. All the people who told her to stay away from that wild Declan Gates and his whole crazy family.

She and Declan hadn't cared. They just kept their friendship a secret, something no one else could touch and spoil.

Until she'd ruined it.

"I'm so sorry, Declan."

"For being so beautiful? You should be. Break a man's heart, you could."

She knew she was supposed to laugh but she couldn't. "I'm sorry I behaved the way I did. I never stopped caring about you. Never. But somehow that just made me meaner."

She gasped for air as the frigid water splashed around their legs.

"You wanted me so much you had to make sure everyone in town knew you hated me?" A smile tugged at his sensual mouth.

"Yes. I know it doesn't make sense. I felt I had to protect myself."

"From me."

"From me. The me you brought out."

"The *real* Lily." He brushed her left nipple with his thumb and it puckered instantly. Already her hips strained toward him, wanting to feel the perfect, powerful touch of him deep inside her again.

Was this the real Lily? This wanton woman swaying in the waves with her lover, naked in the moonlight.

A feather of fear danced over her skin.

"*My* Lily."

Her fear evaporated as Declan pulled her close and she reveled in the comforting heat of his skin. She stood on tiptoe, her thighs brushing his and her breasts crushed against his chest.

Declan's eyes slid closed and a low moan escaped his lips. "Am I dead?" he murmured. "Because I feel like I'm in paradise."

"If you are, I must be, too." She breathed the words against his skin. The warm night air wrapped around her as the cool water lapped at her feet. Too much sensation, too many conflicting emotions.

"As long as we're here together…" His words evolved into a kiss as fierce and dark as the heaving ocean.

She made love to him in the surf as he lay sprawled on the wet sand, uncaring of the water tickling their toes and skating over their hot skin. Her hands planted on his broad chest, she moved over him, her rhythm strong and sure.

She reveled in the dark mystery of the sensations pouring over them like the sharp salt water, in the roughness of his skin and the coarse sand under them, the harsh, raw newness of her feelings.

She had no one to answer to, nothing to prove, only a new universe of awareness to explore.

Declan understood her at a soul-deep level far removed from the habitual, politeness-laced interactions she shared with other people.

He always had.

Was it only with him that she could be the *real* Lily?

Again they climaxed at the exact same moment—hard and fast—and fell together, breathless and gasping onto the damp sand.

Lily's blood roared with excitement. She'd never felt so dangerously, fully and powerfully alive as she did right now in Declan's wet and sandy arms under the almost full moon. The truth of it thrilled her and appalled her in equal measure.

"You'll get cold." Declan gathered her in his arms.

"Cold? This must be the hottest night on record, I don't think I've ever felt so…" Her skin heated again, this time with a blush.

"Aroused?"

She bit her lip. "Crazy." An alarming thought occurred to her. "Where are our clothes?"

Declan shrugged. He looked deliciously natural with his athletic physique dressed in nothing but sand and glistening beads of salt water. If he told her he was really a selkie, who slipped back into the ocean each night after walking in daylight as a man, she wouldn't be the least bit surprised.

He seemed as much a part of the harsh craggy landscape as the dark granite cliffs that rose around them. It was wrong that he'd been gone so long.

"Did you miss Blackrock?" She whispered the question over the rasp of the surf.

Declan looked at her. "No." He spoke without hesitation. The single word cut her like a knife. Then his gaze softened. "But now I'm back, something about the place is starting to get under my skin."

Lily pressed herself against his warm skin and shivered with relief, letting go of her fear and misgivings. Right now, Declan's reassuring embrace was the only place she could stand to be.

Five

Lily awoke to find Declan staring at her. Morning sunlight played in his unruly black hair. A gull soared overhead.

She never made it home because she'd fallen asleep, exhausted, after…

Making love with Declan Gates. A throb of recall heated her insides.

She licked her lips and drew in a breath as a mix of arousal and anxiety tingled in her belly.

"Morning, Lily." His familiar voice sounded gruff yet cheerful.

She groped for a platitude, but no sound came to her lips. She became slowly aware that she lay on something very soft, wrapped in delicious warmth.

"Blankets." The word shot out of her mouth.

"I brought some down from the house." Declan's relaxed expression was even more disconcerting than the open-air awakening.

He lay propped next to her on one elbow, his tan biceps only inches from her face. She could smell the salty musk of his skin. His body heat mingled with hers inside their soft cocoon.

"You fell asleep and you looked so peaceful I didn't want to wake you. I carried you up onto this ledge."

Lily glanced to the side and saw they were on a granite ledge about ten feet above the beach, out of reach of the spray and waves.

She inhaled a lungful of sea air, trying to get her bearings. She remembered the gleaming rows of bottles of distilled liquor, taking a sip from the silver cup…their kiss.

And the rest…

Her memories were a wild jumble of intense sensations and feelings that still quivered in her skin, heated her breasts and thighs and reverberated deep inside her.

She couldn't even blame inebriation for her outrageous behavior—she'd only had one sip.

"I always said you were wild." Declan's gray eyes glimmered with the hint of a smile.

She shoved a hand into her hair, a wild tangle. She'd completely lost control. Abandoned it—*to Declan*.

She drew in a long slow breath as alarm gathered in her brain.

Had he planned this?

He had been so…accommodating. He hadn't made

a fuss about her redecorating his house. He'd broken into the basement for her. He'd helped her carry the bottles without a word of complaint.

Then with a glance of those silver eyes, a dare and a fierce kiss, he'd seduced her in the moonlight and stripped her bare in the splashing surf.

The wicked smile playing about his arrogant mouth made her shrink into the warmth of the blankets.

"No regrets, now, Lily." His voice carried a hint of warning.

He reached out a muscled forearm and brushed his thumb over her lips. Her skin thrilled at his touch, even as fear and misgivings surged inside her.

"I read that you're taking your company public." His eyes narrowed against the rising sun.

She swallowed. "Yes," she rasped.

"Are you doing that just to raise the money to buy this house?" He raised a dark brow and withdrew his arm back under the blankets.

"It was a strategic decision to grow my business to the next level." Her clipped protest sounded foolish under the very unbusinesslike circumstances.

"I see." A smile played about his lips. "You do realize that going public makes you…vulnerable."

His low voice lingered on the last word. Lily shivered under the thick blanket, suddenly feeling vulnerable in every possible way.

"It's a little scary to give up total control…" She paused, realizing how her comments on going public so closely echoed the events of last night.

Declan's feral grin widened.

She cleared her throat and ignored the thickening in her belly. "It'll be a new experience having investors to answer to, but I want to expand the business and this is the best way to raise the capital."

"And the best way to cough up the lavish sum I want for the old family pile." He tilted his head and a black lock dipped seductively to his eyes.

"That, too." She lifted her chin, determined to resist his flirting. "And the factory. In some ways, that's even more important."

"I still don't understand why you want the old mill. Wouldn't it be more cost effective to build a new one?"

"It's a special place." She spoke softly, half-afraid to share her dreams with someone who could crush them beneath his callused palm.

"You could have fooled me. I guess I remember it back when it was belching out soot and sulfur. You must have a powerful vision."

"I do."

His expression turned innocent, curious. "Will you show it to me?"

"The mill or my vision?" Anxiety tightened her muscles.

"Both." He tilted his head. "I suspect it would be educational for me."

She blinked and tried not to frown. "Okay."

Declan didn't try to shower with Lily, though the thought of hot water rolling over her smooth skin made him hard all over again. Instead, he listened from the adjoining bedroom, enjoying the splash and trickle of the water as it poured over her supple curves.

He'd done it.

He'd seduced Lily Wharton.

In fact, calling it a seduction was an exaggeration. She'd torn his clothes off and made love to him with a ferocity he'd never have dared to imagine.

He drew in a long, slow breath.

Victory.

Or at least that's how it should feel.

He rolled his shoulders to dislodge an uneasy tension creeping along his spine.

The woman I always wanted more than anything in the world.

A line. But why not? It was the damn truth, wasn't it?

Making love to Lily Wharton should feel like a climactic moment of triumph. The fulfillment of all his teenage fantasies. The end of an era.

Instead it felt dangerously like—

A beginning.

He sprang off the bed and tugged on the pants he'd brought up from his car.

This was not a beginning, it was an ending. Lily's fondest wish was to take back what he owned of Blackrock. It was entirely possible that cavorting in the waves with him was simply part of *her* cunning plan.

How far would she go to get what she wanted? As he'd observed, her determination was unrivaled.

Except perhaps by his.

* * *

"Now, if we run into my mother…" Lily fluffed her hair as they stepped out into the sunshine. "Remember I told her on the phone that I drove into Bangor and stayed there, okay?"

Declan fought a smile. "A little subterfuge only makes our dangerous liaison more exciting." He opened the passenger door of his silver roadster, already salivating at the prospect of her long, slim, strong legs stepping inside and lowering her luscious form into the glove-leather seats.

"Oh, no, I'll take my car." She gestured at the rusting white station wagon parked next to his.

Declan raised a brow. "You never would ride on the back of my bike, but surely this is enough of a chariot even for Queen Lily?" He admired the sleek silver perfection of his new baby. This car was *fine*.

"Really, it'll be more convenient." She tugged open one of her huge, clunky doors. "This car is my mom's. I have to get it back to the house, and I'm sure we'll want to go our separate ways after we stop at the mill. I usually come up on the train so she lets me drive hers when I'm here."

"Fine." He cursed his pathetic boyish desire to show off his new wheels. As if Lily would care.

She must be worth several million in nonliquid assets but she was so self-possessed it wouldn't occur to her to be embarrassed by driving an old rattletrap.

Typical WASP arrogance.

Damn, he loved that about her.

Her eyes shone. "To see people doing meaningful work, creating quality products in a harmonious environment?"

He couldn't help notice the spring in her step as she marched toward the giant vat where trees were once boiled into malodorous porridge. "Over here, where the digester is now, I want to create a comfortable area for people to take breaks, eat lunch—"

"Compose classical music on handcrafted instruments." He couldn't help himself.

She narrowed her eyes and crossed her arms over her very lovely chest. "If they want to, absolutely. And there's no need to be snarky about it."

She bent over and brushed at the debris at her feet. He allowed himself to enjoy the lush curve of the firm and silky backside he knew was hiding under her rumpled khakis.

"This floor is made from two-inch-thick boards of black locust. Imagine what it will look like when it's sanded and polished."

"A wood floor in a pulp mill? It's a wonder they didn't run it through the chipper."

"It's an honest-to-God miracle, isn't it?" She fixed those bright honey eyes on him. "This factory was originally built to make whalebone corsets, if you can believe that. It's had a few different identities in its time. It's a special place, can't you feel it?"

A prickling surge of heat roamed over Declan's skin as he tried to resist the fierce energy of the formidable Lily Wharton.

Shards of golden light streamed in through broken

chinks high in the old window panes and cast a cheery glow onto the old brick walls. "Yes. I wish I couldn't, but I can."

"This factory was probably the reason the town grew here in the first place."

"And you're going to turn it back into Blackrock's beating heart."

"You can mock me. I don't care." She brushed her hands off on her pants. "As long as you sell it to me."

She headed back toward the door, her graceful stride carrying her over the rubble like a gliding angel.

Declan shook his head. She was right, damn it. This space could be spectacular, and her vision for bringing employment back to the town, which had a tradition of hard-working and loyal employees…

Lily. Lily. Lily. Why did she have to be so perfect? Beautiful, brainy and as fierce and unrelenting as a thunderstorm.

If he didn't know better, he'd almost think he could fall in love with a woman like that.

Lucky thing his heart had long ago been pulped down to a paper husk.

Lily was already climbing into her car by the time he got outside.

"Leaving so soon? It's been ten years since I visited Blackrock. Won't you show me around the town? I'd like to see what's changed."

Lily paused, obviously flustered. "Um. I don't think much has changed at all."

"Don't want to be seen walking the streets with Declan Gates?" He tipped his head and surveyed her through narrowed eyes.

"Don't be ridiculous."

"What then? It's Saturday. You can't be in a rush to get to work."

"I do have a lot to do." She tucked a strand of hair behind her ear.

"So much that you can't spare half an hour to reminisce with an old friend?" He feigned a polite smile.

He watched her chest rise as she drew in a breath. "Oh, I suppose I can spare a few minutes, though I can't imagine you'll see anything of interest to you."

"Oh, I'm quite sure I will." He let his gaze drift to the swell of her breasts inside her demure cotton shirt. He knew how readily those nipples would thicken under his touch.

Lily raised her chin and walked toward the gate. "Which way?"

"How about the school?" He spoke slowly, watching for her reaction. "I don't think we ever went there together."

He saw Lily startle. The thrill of making her uncomfortable was undercut by the painful truth that she apparently still didn't want to go there with him. Which only made him more determined. "Come on." He held out his arm. Lily glanced down the street warily.

No one in sight.

Declan held his arm steady, and she reluctantly took it.

He could almost hear lace curtains twitching aside

behind the windows of the modest frame houses lining the inappropriately named and inconveniently steep Commercial Street. He strode with confidence, determined to mine this moment for every wicked thrill he could get out of it.

Lily's long legs matched his stride for stride along the sidewalk. She stared ahead, presenting him with her proud profile as he enjoyed the sensual jostle of her arm and waist against his.

He'd been so sure he'd never see this town again. He certainly never imagined he'd be back here walking arm in arm with Lily Wharton down the town's main street in broad daylight.

He shot her a smile that might have seemed menacing had she turned to acknowledge it. But she didn't.

They turned onto Draper Street and the familiar pale brick building of Blackrock High came into sight. "The New School." He spoke aloud, enjoying the strangeness of the situation.

Their alma mater had been rebuilt in the 1950s to accommodate Blackrock's baby boom and the name had stuck.

Much like the reputation he'd been tarred with.

Two older women pushing grocery carts came into view. One of them waved at Lily. The other peered at him through plastic-rimmed glasses.

Declan felt Lily's arm stiffen as they drew closer. "Mrs. Ramsay, how's your ankle doing?"

"Mending fine, thank you, Lily." The woman's eyes never left Declan. She raised a salt-and-pepper brow. "Aren't you going to introduce us to your gentleman friend?"

Lily cleared her throat. "I'm sure you don't need an introduction. You remember Declan Gates?" Her voice only quavered a little as she said his name.

The woman's smile vanished. "I thought he was dead." Her hand flew to her mouth. "Excuse my manners, but you've been gone for years and…"

"Purely wishful thinking, I'm afraid." He smiled pleasantly.

He felt Lily's gaze boring into him and he decided to try a different tactic. He glanced at the second woman, who looked the same as he remembered her from ten years ago, complete with disapproving frown. "Hello, Mrs. Miller. I used to buy supplies for my bike at your husband's garage. How's he doing?"

"Died of a stroke three years ago," she hissed through pursed lips.

"I'm sorry to hear that. He was quite a mentor to me."

"I'm sure." Mrs. Miller's mouth settled into a hard line.

Declan struggled to keep his feet on the high road as an awkward silence settled over their little group. Lily's arm—still thrust bravely in his—filled him with strange and conflicting emotions.

"I'm glad to hear your ankle's mending," said Lily brightly, only a slight strain in her voice. "We're off to see the school."

"Attendance is down." Mrs. Ramsay adjusted her watch strap on her thick wrist. "Not sure how long it'll stay open. What with the mill being gone, and all." She drew the last words out, staring right past Lily and Declan, along the empty street. "Well, I must be off. I have my shopping to do."

"Of course. Nice to see you." Lily nodded politely at them. Declan just stared.

When they were out of earshot he leaned into Lily. "I'm impressed you kept your arm in mine."

"Why shouldn't I have?" She shot him a fierce look.

"Tongues will be wagging." He flicked his tongue over his lips.

Lily glanced away. "It may shock you to know that people have more interesting things to think about than what you're doing back in town. I don't know what got into those two, they're usually very friendly."

Declan knew exactly what had got into them—prejudice against him. Shame old Mr. Miller was dead. He was one of the few people in town he could have an actual conversation with.

A tall, slender man in black approached along the sidewalk. Declan recognized him as the local vicar who'd tried—and failed miserably—to involve his mother in some charitable activities.

"Hi, Reverend!" Lily called out. "How are things going with the church bazaar?"

Reverend Peake's eyes fixed on Declan and widened.

"Fine, fine, must run." The man picked up his pace as he strode toward them.

"Do you need me to… Oh." Lily pursed her lips as he whipped past them. "How odd."

"Only because you're not used to it."

"What do you mean?"

"The Declan Gates treatment. They don't come out and insult me—my family was too powerful for them to take that kind of risk. They don't want to bite the hand that feeds them. No, they all back away from me as if *I* might bite."

He stared along the steep, narrow street. "Like I'm a horned devil in their midst. Appropriate considering

the invigorating smell of sulfur that used to fill these streets." He raised an eyebrow. "Don't pretend this is a surprise. You used to treat me just the same."

Lily paused and drew her arm out of his. Her wide hazel eyes stared into his face with such force he almost had to shift position.

Then she turned to look beyond the rooftops, to where the vast ocean shimmered. When she turned back her expression was resolute.

"You're right. I'm *ashamed*." Her voice rose on the last word and color brightened her cheeks. She glanced up and down the street. "I can't believe it never seemed shocking to me before."

"Because you bought into it. Part of you wanted to accept what your parents and friends and all the people you looked up to were saying.

"Even though you knew me—really knew me—you still needed to believe the evil Gates family was destroying your precious Blackrock. That the dangerous and wild Gates brothers threatened the virginity of every girl in the town."

He narrowed his eyes. "Perhaps there was some truth to that last one, at least if rumors are to be believed."

He let a wry smile twist his lips, hiding the anger that surged within him when he remembered how he and
his brothers were treated. No surprise he'd cherished a fantasy of the house and the town falling forgotten into the dark ocean.

A woman pushing a baby carriage looked over at them as she walked along the opposite side of the street. Declan recognized her as one of their classmates. She squinted at him for a second, then stared, open-mouthed.

Declan raised his hand to wave, admittedly issuing a challenge rather than a friendly salute. His former classmate's mouth snapped shut and she continued up the hill, pushing the stroller at a brisk pace.

"Ella!" Lily called to her, but she'd already disappeared around the nearest corner.

She raised wide, shiny eyes to his. "It must have been horrible for you."

He shrugged and hoped the ugly memories didn't show on his face. "What doesn't kill you...you know?"

Lily shoved a hand through her blond hair. "I feel terrible."

"Guilt is a waste of time. What happened happened. I probably wouldn't be as driven and successful as I am today if I'd had a happy childhood."

"I have a confession to make." Color drained from Lily's face. She glanced up and down the street. Her eyes fixed on his, wide and wary. "I don't know if it's a good idea to tell you this or not. Probably not." She licked her lips. "But I have to."

She stared at him for a moment with those big, honey eyes. "I started a rumor about you."

He lifted his chin and kept a poker face. "I hope it was a good one."

Lily's drew in a breath. "You know that scandal about how you got a girl pregnant?"

"Sure. I think I read that one on the locker-room wall, among other places." He shoved his hands in his pockets, determined not to feel anything at all.

"It was my fault." She rubbed a hand over her mouth. "My mom had begun to suspect there was something between us." She sucked in a shaky breath. "It was right after you kissed me. She accused me of being…friendly with you. I…I…I told her it was nonsense and made up the rumor to make it seem like I hated you." Lily twisted her hands together.

Declan's heart squeezed and he couldn't stop the surge of fury that heated his blood. "Who the hell was I supposed to get pregnant when there wasn't a girl in Blackrock who'd come within twenty paces of me?"

She shook her head. "It was a stupid, thoughtless thing to do. I just said it on the spur of the moment. I had no idea she'd tell someone and it would spread. I'm so sorry."

"There was only *one* girl I wanted." His anger rang in his voice.

"I know." Tears sprang to her eyes. "I know…" Her voice trailed off in a whisper. "But you could have denied the rumor. Why didn't you ever deny it?"

"Would anyone have believed me if I had?"

A gull screamed above them and Lily wiped at her eyes with the back of her hand.

Declan held himself steady. The strong urge to comfort her fought with disbelief and deep hurt that *she'd* been the one who started the vile rumor that blackened his name.

She'd erected his scandalous reputation as a wall between them and followed her family's hateful advice to shun him.

He shook his head. "Maybe you shouldn't have told me, Lily."

"You will still sell me the factory and the house, won't you?" She fixed her piercing gaze on him, eyes still bright with tears. "You wouldn't hold a grudge, not after all these years?"

He blew out a burst of air. "That's what it all comes down to, isn't it? Nothing can interfere with your grand plan. Just like you didn't want to upset the applecart by being friends with a Gates, or risk your precious status by kissing Dangerous Declan."

He stepped toward her, crowded her. Her distinctive natural scent, like wildflowers in the rain, taunted him.

"What would the good people of Blackrock think if they knew you gave yourself to me, naked in the waves last night?"

He spoke low, keeping the conversation private. Was he so wrapped up in Lily even he couldn't help but play her games, keep her secrets?

Lily lifted her chin. "We both got carried away."

A laugh rumbled low in his chest. "Maybe you got carried away, my lovely Lily." He narrowed his eyes. "Not me. My grand plan is a little different from yours, you see."

He saw the panic start in her eyes. It socked him in the gut how little she trusted him, even though that was his explicit intention. "Don't fret, Lily, I'll still sell to you."

Her shoulders softened and an expression of relief crossed her beautiful face. "Thank you, Declan."

The words sounded like manna from heaven drifting from those soft pink lips. Declan steeled himself against the allure of the one woman who could destroy all his defenses.

"Don't thank me yet." He tipped his head back and thrust his chin at her. "Because I won't lower my price. It stands at ten million dollars."

He turned and strode back to his car. No doubt she was relieved to be rid of him and the discomfort he brought.

He'd been tempted to declare that frolicking in the surf with him had failed to bring her any closer to her goal of reclaiming Blackrock—which would only have confirmed her opinion that he lacked even a shred of decency.

Of course, she'd have been right.

If Blackrock crumbled and fell into the sea, he wouldn't spill any salt tears in after it.

Six

Lily's heart almost stopped when she saw the headline of the *Blackrock Courier*.

"Textilecom makes offer on Gates Mill." She snatched the rustling pages from her mother and slapped them down on the breakfast table. "The Ohio-based manufacturing giant has plans to purchase the abandoned Victorian structure on Commercial Street. A Textilecom spokesman confirmed the company's interest in the former pulp mill, possibly for conversion to a wallpaper plant."

The text jumbled before her disbelieving eyes. "I don't understand. Why would one of the biggest textile manufacturers in the world want to hijack my plans for this space? Sure, they probably consider me a rival on some very minor level, but how did they even hear of Blackrock?"

"I don't like to talk about people behind their back." Her mother rose from the table, carrying her cup. "But when you told me Declan Gates turned up here like a bad penny, I warned you no good could come of it."

Lily sat back in her chair, gasping for breath. "You think Declan sought them out and encouraged their interest in the property?"

Her mother shrugged as she poured herself another cup of coffee. "Maybe once he knew you were interested, he decided to see if he could drum up some competition and raise the price?"

"Declan wouldn't do that."

Don't fret, Lily, I'll still sell to you.

The look in his eyes, strangely vulnerable, a flashback to the Declan she'd been so close to, had reassured her that he meant it.

"Don't tell me you believe a word that good-for-nothing troublemaker says. When Rita Miller told me she'd seen the two of you in town—arm in arm!—I couldn't believe my ears. Why, you told me yourself the boy had no scruples. That he…" Her mother paused and sipped her coffee, possibly wondering if discretion really was the better part of valor.

"That he what, Mom?" Lily's stomach tightened. She knew the answer.

She still hadn't brought herself to tell anyone that the rumor she'd inadvertently started was a bold-faced lie.

Perhaps she was afraid the next thing off her tongue would be an admission that she'd made unbridled love to him under the moonlight.

Though why exactly did she feel the need to keep their tryst a secret?

"You told me that Declan Gates engaged in... *intercourse*." She emphasized the word with a throaty rasp. "With a young girl." Her mother raised a slim, gray brow.

"It's not true." Heat rose to Lily's face. "Declan was a perfect gentleman." Her knife and fork clattered to her plate. "I'm going to tell you the truth. I made up that story. I made it up because Declan and I *were* friends, Mom. There's something really twisted about the fact that I felt I had to keep that secret from you."

Her mother's face tightened. "I always suspected something. Then when I accused you, you denied it."

"You put me on the spot!"

"You lied to me."

Lily licked her lips and drew in a shaky breath. "I did. I'm ashamed of that. I'm disgusted by how my cowardice has hurt Declan and I'm not going to lie anymore."

Her mother's eyes narrowed. "I noticed the way you'd sneak out of the house after school. Did you ever have sex with Declan Gates?"

"No!" She spat the word, hot to defend Declan's ill-deserved reputation as a womanizer.

Then her face heated as she realized she'd just told another brazen lie.

"I never did anything with Declan back then."

Except kiss him.

"And he never tried to do anything with me. I treated him shamefully." Her chair scraped as she rose from the table, heart pounding.

Her mother glanced down at the paper on the table. "And apparently now he's decided to take his revenge."

Revenge? Lily frowned. Was it possible?

My grand plan is a little different from yours.

Declan's words echoed in her brain.

Perhaps even making love to her had been…

No, her mind couldn't even comprehend that he'd have seduced her purely out of spite. Their lovemaking had been tender and cautious, strange, yes, but long-awaited and heartfelt and…beautiful.

"Lily, you look white as a ghost. You really must stop working so hard."

Lily had almost forgotten her mother was in the room.

"I'm fine. I have to go find out what's going on with this Textilecom thing. They're famous for paying low wages and exploiting workers. Them moving here would be a disaster for Blackrock."

"First, I think you should read the rest of the article. It may dispel any romantic notions you still harbor about your *old friend* Declan Gates."

The following weekend, Lily lurched the old station wagon back into first gear to get enough juice for the climb up the steep and winding driveway to the house.

She'd seen a light on in the window, which meant one thing. Declan was there.

She'd tried to call him all week, only to be told he was traveling in Asia. After a week of dealing with clients and vendors and financial advisors preparing her IPO—all without a word from Declan—her nerves were in tatters.

The article in the Blackrock paper had outlined Declan's meteoric rise to prominence as a rogue investor who saw potential and profits where no one else did. He'd made his first fortune scavenging the ruins of the dot.com era. He'd grown his profits and his reputation as a hawk by swooping down on ailing companies and breaking them apart for sale, usually to their closest local competitor.

Lily pulled into the gravel turnaround and brought the car to a stop.

Did he plan to destroy her company and raid it for spare parts the way he had with First Electronics, Lang Semiconductor and the rest of them? Most of his business activity was in Asia, which explained why it was news to her.

After the shocking article about Declan and his plans to sell to Textilecom, she'd called the *Blackrock Courier*—a valiant publishing effort run out of the church basement—and given the editor an interview about her goals.

A long-time town resident, the editor had attempted to get her to say some unkind things about Declan, and she had made a point of doing just the opposite. "I'm sure he only wants what's best for the town."

The wishful thought sounded laughable in retrospect,

but if anyone in town hated Declan afresh, she didn't want it to be because of words that emerged from her mouth.

Her printed insistence that she—not Textilecom—would be buying the Blackrock mill had since been turned into an Old West–style wrangle by some business blogs, and by Wednesday the story had hit the inner pages of the *New York Times* and the *Wall Street Journal.*

The entire situation, including the future of Blackrock, was in Declan's hands, and he hadn't even bothered to return her call.

But apparently he had decided to come up and visit for the weekend, as she'd heard through the grapevine almost as soon as his flashy sports car purred into town.

She drew in a long, slow breath, trying to calm her nerves. Despite her better judgment she glanced in the mirror and fluffed her limp hair. She'd opened the door and stepped one foot out into the gathering darkness when the wide front door flung open.

Declan stood there, his white shirt gleaming in the dusk. "I knew you'd come."

"I'm sorry to be so predictable." She slammed the car door and strode to the steps. "But you don't seem to be reachable by phone."

"I couldn't talk to *you* on the phone, Lily." He leaned on the doorframe, broad shoulders silhouetted against the light. "You're too dangerous. You'd wrap me up in all those slick words of yours." He stood aside and gestured for her to enter. She caught a glimpse of the feral gleam in his eye. "I need you where I can *smell* you."

His voice, thick with suggestion, rasped close to her

ear. She shivered as her body responded immediately, her nipples tightening inside her blouse.

She turned to face him. His expression of boyish mischief only enhanced the raw desire she saw reflected in his gray eyes.

His gaze slid over her neck, hovered around her breasts, then trailed down the length of her legs to her sturdy pumps.

"I'm surprised that my practical business attire is so riveting." She tried to project a calm she wasn't feeling.

Declan's mouth hitched into a slight smile. "It's not the clothes that are riveting. It's what's underneath them. You'll recall I'm now very familiar with your personal terrain."

"I could say the same." She lifted her chin. Declan was also still in his work clothes, sans tie. Two could play at this game.

She dropped her eyes to where his shirt collar lay unbuttoned, revealing the strip of bare skin and sprinkling of black hair at his throat.

Heat gathered low in her belly as she let her gaze wander over the crisp cotton of his shirt. It was impossible not to remember the thick, taut muscle wound tightly beneath it.

A smile flitted across her lips when she glanced below his black leather belt. "Happy to see me, huh?"

His arousal bulged indelicately against the fine wool of his pants.

"I'm always happy to see you, my lovely Lily."

The possessive edge to his words *should* make her mad.

But Declan's voice rang with a deep conviction that assured her—possibly in spite of his own wishes—that he really was happy to see her.

And damn her if she wasn't happy to see him.

It was all she could do to keep a smile from ripping across her face. She should be boiling with rage! How did he still do this to her?

"Drink?"

"Um, no, thanks." She struggled to collect her scattered thoughts and get back on track before she wound up unbuttoning his shirt again. "You know why I'm here. What are you doing with Textilecom?"

Declan's brows lowered. "Still putting business before pleasure, I see."

"This whole situation may be a joke to you, Declan, but I assure you that the future of this town is no laughing matter for the people around here."

"Textilecom made me a very interesting offer."

"How did they hear about the factory?"

Declan narrowed his eyes. "You think I tipped them off?"

"The thought did cross my mind." She crossed her arms over her chest, ignoring the sting in her nipples.

"I'm disappointed that you have such a low opinion of me. I thought we'd turned over a new leaf in the long and colorful history of our relationship."

Lily started at the word *relationship.* Did Declan think their wild tryst in the waves might be the start of something?

A fierce rushing sensation flooded her limbs.

"I… We did. In fact, I told my mother I'd lied about that rumor." She cocked her chin at him, embarrassed by how childish her protest sounded. "I even told the papers you're a good person, that you had the best interests of the town at heart.…" Her garbled words sounded like meaningless chatter under his piercing stare.

"I don't care about them. Did *you* think I'd sell the factory out from under you?"

She swallowed. "No… I don't know. Maybe I did. I don't know you anymore, Declan. From the things you said when we parted, about your grand scheme being different from mine, I don't know what to think."

She could have lied and told him what he wanted to hear—that she trusted him—but given their past, she owed him honesty, even if the consequences were harsher.

Declan's expression hardened. "You're right to be wary. It puts you in good company."

She shivered, remembering all the articles detailing Declan's ruthless business dealings. He must have made a lot of enemies.

"So are you going to sell to them, or not?"

An odd expression flickered over Declan's face— surprise? Then it closed into an unreadable mask. "I guess we'll have to see who's still standing after the dust settles."

Her hackles shot up. "You intend to encourage this competition for the property?"

"I don't intend to do anything at all. Right now you don't have the money to buy it, Textilecom does."

She gasped. "But I'm taking my company public to raise the cash, you know that." Her voice rose to a squawk.

She took a deep breath and tried to regain some composure. "I'll be more than able to pay you."

Declan raised a dark brow. "So you say."

Fear unfurled along her spine. "Do you know something I don't know?"

His expression remained infuriatingly enigmatic. "How would I know anything? I specialize in electronics and rarely invest outside Asia."

A rumble of fury stirred in Lily's chest at his callous attitude. Especially in light of the explicit intimacy they'd shared only one week ago.

That night she'd seen a glimpse of the old Declan. The real Declan. She knew his warm and loving core was still in there, burning like a red hot coal inside the cool exterior of the ruthless businessman before her.

Even now she could imagine his hands on her skin, firm and insistent, yet cautious and caring.

"Declan." She stretched out her hand, hoping to reach past the wall of ice he'd erected around himself.

He surveyed her hand as if it was a curiosity. Then he lifted it in his own and brought it to his lips.

The pressure of his thumb on her palm took her breath away. Her eyelids shivered closed as he pressed his warm lips to the back of her hand, brushing the tender skin.

Heat suffused her body, and her skin hummed inside her conservative suit.

Her knees trembled when he gently turned her hand

over and lowered his mouth over the soft skin of her palm. His tongue caressed the heart line and sent a shimmer of desire shooting through her that emerged from her mouth as a slight moan.

The sound yanked her attention out of the fog of lust Declan had lulled her into.

She snatched her hand back. "I will raise the money for the property."

They were the wrong words.

She wanted to say so much more. She wanted to take back the pain she'd caused him, all the bitterness that had poisoned him against her and Blackrock.

She wanted to make it right, to heal the legacy of hatred and ugliness her heartless actions had caused.

And most of all, she wanted to take him in her arms and hold him—*tight*—until words became meaningless and even thoughts fell away.

But Declan's diamond-hard stare made that impossible. His lips straightened into a line that matched the stubborn set of his jaw. His pale eyes glittered with emotion that had nothing to do with affection, or tenderness or fond memories of good times shared together.

"Maybe you will, maybe you won't." He surveyed her with those cool, gray eyes. "I've lived on this earth too long to believe in promises. Words are just words. It's actions that count."

Lily shrank under the renewed accusation that she'd acted poorly all those years ago. She'd been selfish and insensitive. Untrustworthy.

She swallowed. "This time I won't let you down. I'll

Get FREE BOOKS and FREE GIFTS when you play the...

LAS VEGAS

GAME

Just scratch off
the gold box with a coin.
Then check below to see
the gifts you get!

YES! I have scratched off the gold box. Please send
me my **2 FREE BOOKS** and **2 FREE GIFTS** for which I qualify. I
understand that I am under no obligation to purchase any
books as explained on the back of this card.

▼ DETACH AND MAIL CARD TODAY! ▼

326 SDL ENXG

225 SDL ENN5

FIRST NAME

LAST NAME

ADDRESS

APT.#

CITY

STATE/PROV.

ZIP/POSTAL CODE

(S-D-01/08)

7	7	7	Worth TWO FREE BOOKS plus TWO FREE GIFTS!
🍒	🍒	🍒	Worth TWO FREE BOOKS!
♣	♣	♣	TRY AGAIN!

www.eHarlequin.com

Offer limited to one per household and not
valid to current subscribers of Silhouette
Desire®. All orders subject to approval.

© 2007 HARLEQUIN ENTERPRISES LIMITED
® and ™ are trademarks owned and used by the trademark owner and/or its licensee.

Your Privacy - Silhouette Books is committed to protecting your privacy. Our privacy policy is available online at
www.eHarlequin.com or upon request from the Silhouette Reader Service. From time to time we make our lists
of customers available to reputable third parties who may have a product or service of interest to you. If you
would prefer for us not to share your name and address, please check here. ☐

The Silhouette Reader Service — Here's how it works:

Accepting your 2 free books and 2 free gifts (gifts valued at approximately $10.00) places you under no obligation to buy anything. You may keep the books and gifts and return the shipping statement marked "cancel." If you do not cancel, abou a month later we'll send you 6 additional books and bill you just $4.05 each in the U.S. or $4.74 each in Canada, plus 25¢ shipping and handling per book and applicable taxes if any.* That's the complete price and — compared to cover prices o $4.75 each in the U.S. and $5.75 each in Canada — it's quite a bargain! You may cancel at any time, but if you choose to continue, every month we'll send you 6 more books, which you may either purchase at the discount price or return to us and cancel your subscription.

*Terms and prices subject to change without notice. Sales tax applicable in N.Y. Canadian residents will be charged applicable provincial taxes and GST. Credit or debit balances in a customer's account(s) may be offset by any other outstanding balance owed by or to the customer. Please allow 4 to 6 weeks for delivery. Offer available while quantities las

If offer card is missing, write to: Silhouette Reader Service, 3010 Walden Ave., P.O. Box 1867, Buffalo NY 14240-1867

BUSINESS REPLY MAIL

FIRST-CLASS MAIL   PERMIT NO. 717   BUFFALO, NY

POSTAGE WILL BE PAID BY ADDRESSEE

SILHOUETTE READER SERVICE
3010 WALDEN AVE
PO BOX 1867
BUFFALO NY 14240-9952

NO POSTAGE
NECESSARY
IF MAILED
IN THE
UNITED STATES

make good on my word. In the meantime, please don't sell to Textilecom." The pleading edge to her voice angered her. So unprofessional.

But how could she be professional around a man who'd made her give up every last vestige of control? Who'd taken her to heights of pleasure—of madness— she couldn't have imagined if she tried.

"I'll make my decisions based on what is best for my bottom line, not on what's best for Lily Wharton."

His low voice betrayed no emotion. No hint of what they'd shared on the beach.

Her hand still hummed with the sensual touch of his lips. The desire to reach out—to really touch him, beyond the physical—ached in her heart.

How could he be so cold? So cruel?

"You've changed, Declan." Her words rang off the polished wood floor and the grand oak staircase. Low and filled with conviction, her voice gave her confidence to spill the words overflowing her heart.

"You've always had a reputation for being bad." She took a step toward him. "And, if we're being honest here, it wasn't entirely undeserved. You never cared what anyone thought of you, so it's no wonder that they didn't always think the best. You always thought rules were for other people, you didn't give a hang about being on time, or prepared or even clean."

Of course, she could blame his uncaring mother, but still…

She forged ahead, her convictions gathering steam as her voice filled the majestic hallway around them. "How do you think the teachers felt when you failed to bring in your homework, day after day?"

Though, he *had* gone on to Yale....

"Did it ever occur to you that my parents might have had good reason to worry about me being off alone in the woods with you?"

He blinked. The first sign that he was even paying attention. "I'd never have hurt you, Lily."

"I knew that, but how would they? You *were* wild, Declan. In a good way to a great extent, but you can't blame everyone else for the way they looked down on you. You were different."

Her words rang off the dark slate floor. Light from the adjoining room cast harsh shadows across Declan's chiseled face in the deepening gloom of dusk.

"You've changed. The old Declan would never have been deliberately cruel. That's what you're being now, by threatening to sell to Textilecom. Why would you do that if not to hurt me?"

She shook her head and blew out a breath. "You wouldn't hurt a fly back then—literally! You'd have captured it and studied it and played with it, then you'd have put it back exactly where you found it so it could go about its little fly business."

She ignored the way his sooty lashes lowered over those glittering diamond eyes. If he thought he could flirt his way out of this he was very much mistaken.

"That was the *old* Declan. I thought he was still inside you. I thought that warmhearted and wild boy was hidden down there under that expensive suit, but now I know different.

"You used to irritate the heck out of everyone in town with that roaring motorcycle engine of yours. You didn't care. I'll admit it now, I used to love that sound. Every time I heard it, my heart leaped and I thought *Declan's here.* We weren't even friends by then, but it made me happy just that you were out there and that you were still…you."

The sun must have slipped behind the horizon as she spoke because she could barely make out Declan's eyes in the gloom.

"I tried so hard not to fall in love with you." She shook her head and a harsh laugh rattled her chest. "I did love you, I suppose, though I wouldn't have known to use that word for it back then." She stiffened her spine and drew in a shaky breath. "But I won't make that mistake again."

She took a step back, hoping she could find her way to the door in the dark. "Because after today, I know that boy I once knew is gone for good. He's *dead.*"

The heated words peeled off her tongue like flames. "Yes, you used to be a motorcycle-riding bad boy with a worse reputation, but at least you had a soul. Maybe you should get back on your bike and go look for it."

She turned and pushed for the door, heart pounding and blood ringing in her ears.

She didn't need him.

If he wanted to sell to Textilecom just to spite her, so be it. She wasn't going to let him jerk her about like a puppet on strings and drop her in a heap when he was done with her.

She'd been born without the house and the factory, and if it came down to it, she'd live without them, too.

The heavy wood doors opened into deep blue darkness left by the departed sun. A chill in the air snapped at the collar of her silk blouse. She groped to her car in the thin moonlight and scrambled into her seat.

She started the engine, then switched off the annoying love song that crooned from the radio.

A horrible emptiness sank into her as she pulled out of the turnaround and onto the drive. Her heart ached, battered by the way he'd made it burst with something like…hope.

Then crushed it under his heel.

She was far too practical for this craziness. His insolent kiss still burned her palm like a brand, and she rubbed her hand on her thigh to dispel the sensation.

"If I never see Declan Gates again it will be way too soon!" she shouted into the black night, careless of the open windows.

Now, if only she could make herself believe it.

Seven

Declan tried to maintain an edge of righteous anger as Lily's car puttered off into the thick, seaweed-scented night.

He should slam the door and be glad to see the back of her.

She didn't trust him. She'd said the townspeople were right to dislike and fear him. That her parents had been right to protect her from him.

So why couldn't he hate her?

The distant surf crashing on the beach roared in his ears as confusion surged in his brain. He'd set out to seduce her. Done it deliberately. With malice aforethought.

Hadn't he?

He cursed the dull ache in the place where his heart used to be.

Was she right? Had he truly lost his soul?

It was a distinct possibility. He'd survived most of his life by locking away feelings and emotions that could hurt him. By wearing a mask of invincible cool that cowed competitors and won heated battles far quicker than any shouted bluster would.

But was there anything left under the mask?

When he and Lily were young he'd held nothing back. He'd shared his thoughts, his dreams, a piece of his heart. And she'd handed it back to him on a platter.

Since then he'd confided in no one.

Most days his mind dealt with practicalities: price-to-earnings ratios and tangible assets, bridge loans and leveraged buyouts.

Did he even have dreams anymore?

Lily's mention of his motorcycle stuck in his mind. His beloved Kawasaki ZX9. He'd lavished more love, care and blissful hours of fascinated distraction on that bike than on any woman he'd met since Lily.

When he'd left Blackrock he'd stowed it in a corner of the old carriage house, flung a tarp over it and abandoned it without a second glance. Maybe because it represented a part of him he intended to leave behind for good. The impractical Declan who loved to live in the moment, to feel the sea air bite his skin, to roar with the wind along the cliff edge.

He blew out a breath. Damn. Just thinking about it got his adrenaline revving.

Was it still there?

The cool evening breeze crept under his shirt and

made goose bumps rise on his skin. He really should close the front door and go catch up on some reading.

Why did it irk him so much that Lily was mad at him? He'd wanted revenge for the cruel way she'd treated him. Heck, he'd come up here today because he'd read the stories about a struggle for the old Gates factory. It had smelled like a fight and stirred his blood.

He'd been salivating for some intrigue and conflict, eagerly anticipating Lily's flashing eyes and heaving chest.

So why didn't it feel good?

He slipped out into the night and closed the front door quietly behind him. The cool air stung his skin, fresh and invigorating after a week in climate-controlled offices.

Gravel crunched under his feet as he walked toward the hulking shadow of the three-bay carriage house.

This was stupid. Even if the bike were still there, the sea air would have turned it into a mangled heap of rust by now.

Still, he pulled on the heavy, iron door handle and heard the familiar creak of the rusty hinges. The mingled smells of dust, motor oil and mouse greeted his nostrils. Not entirely unpleasant, at least judging by the way his heart rate jumped.

Was that it? He saw a shadowy shape in the far right corner and groped on the wall for the metal light switch. Since the old caretaker still came by once a week, there was an inside chance of the light actually working.

Two bare bulbs snapped on, filling the musty space with yellow light.

It was there.

He strode past the gray-robed hulk of an old car, toward the bundled blue tarp in the corner.

He held his breath, blood pounding as he lifted a corner of the tarp and flung it back.

The sleek black-and-chrome bike greeted him like an old friend. He touched the edge of the low-slung, curved windshield, then ran his hand over the still-shiny black paint. It was a moment before he realized he was holding his breath.

He let it out slowly. So Lily used to like the sound of his engine, huh? The thought made him smile.

He'd loved that sound. It filled his senses, made him feel like he could do anything, go anywhere. So why, when it was time for him to leave Blackrock, had he left the bike behind?

As his eyes grew used to the gloom, he saw the tires were dried and cracked. The rims pitted with specks of rust.

He'd left to travel the world, starting with Asia which had always called out to him. Then he'd gone on to college and business, keeping Blackrock and everything in it squeezed out of his mind.

Maybe he truly had left a part of himself behind when he parked his bike in this dusty corner for the last time.

He knelt to examine the engine and a quick inspection reminded him that he'd taken the time to top up the oil and drain the cooling system. Had he suspected he might come back for it one day?

He shook his head, wishing he'd covered the exposed metal parts with grease to protect them from the harsh salt air.

The flashy white *Ninja* decal on the tail still made him smile, though now he was smiling at his younger self.

So Lily used to think he had soul.

Or had *a* soul. Whatever.

Maybe you should get on your bike and go look for it?

His fingers prickled with anticipation at the thought of seizing the handlebars and mounting the throbbing engine again.

He jumped to his feet, trying to escape a sudden burst of enthusiasm that threatened to make him act a fool.

As if this bike could run after ten years of neglect?

No way. The tires were shot, for one thing.

Of course he could buy new tires at any bike shop.

No. He wasn't going to do this. He had research to do, and phone calls to make now that it was daytime in Hong Kong.

Then again, the fuel tank hadn't rusted and the fuel and brake lines looked okay, at least from the outside.

The chain was well greased and in good working order. He crouched and pinched it between his fingers. Enjoyed the sting of sharp metal against his skin.

Damn if he could ever resist a challenge.

"Mom, can we just drop the subject?"

A peaceful Sunday afternoon and Lily found herself sitting at the dining-room table polishing the silver tea tray with such vigor that it was getting hot.

Like her temper.

Why did her mom always seem to bring out the rebellious teenager in her these days?

"But, darling, you have to have children before you turn thirty. Isn't that when your eggs start to shrivel up?"

Lily gritted her teeth and polished harder. "You didn't have me until you were thirty-two."

"That's because you're the youngest. I'd been married for five years by your age. In my day you'd have been considered an old maid. Look at Katie, she's so happy with the twins, and Robert and Valerie are planning for a third next year."

"Then I'm doing my part to prevent overpopulation." Her siblings had their priorities—adorable ones, admittedly—and she had hers.

"But you never even *date* anyone."

"I've been on dates." Hadn't she? Well, maybe not lately. But she certainly did go out for a lot of business dinners, which was almost the same thing.

And there had been that night with Declan.

She lost her grip on the tray and it clattered onto the walnut dining-room table.

"Watch out!"

"Sorry. Nothing's scratched." She examined the tray. What on earth was the point of a tea tray that needed polishing every ten minutes?

A rumbling noise distracted her attention. "Is Dan mowing the lawn today?"

"Not until Tuesday. But seriously, I talked to Nina Sullivan about getting you together with her son, Jeffrey. He's a podiatrist, you know. Very successful."

"Good for him. I don't have time for dating, Mom."

"You should make time. Get your priorities in order."

Maybe it was a helicopter. Her ears pricked at the sound, straining to hear it over her mother's waxing rhapsodic about a man she knew to be as dull as an unpolished tea tray. Though his bald head certainly was shiny.

The throaty growl grew louder and closer until the window panes started to rattle. There was something eerily familiar about the exact pitch of the noise that made her pulse thud like a drum.

Could it be? She put the tray down and jumped to her feet.

Her scalp tingled as she hurried to the window and peered out through the lace curtains. The air throbbed with sound.

"What is that racket?" her mother snapped. "It sounds like the world is ending."

Lily pushed open the front door and stepped out into the warm late-afternoon sunshine. The rumble of an engine filled her ears and she knew exactly where she'd heard that sound before.

It was Declan's bike.

The aggressive, pulsing roar sent all kinds of strange and terrifying feelings skittering through her.

She'd told him to get back on his bike and go look for his soul.

He'd listened to her. Maybe there was still a human heart beating under that expensive suit?

At that moment the bike roared up her driveway

and screeched to a halt right in front of her with a spray of gravel.

Declan killed the engine, and the silent air throbbed with anticipation. She couldn't help smiling as she watched him lift a broad, denim-clad thigh over the black leather seat and plant it firmly on solid ground.

"Hello, Lily." His deep voice caressed her ears. The wind whipped his black hair.

"You're not wearing a helmet."

"Arrest me." He held out his wrists.

She left the safety of the doorway and stepped toward him. His face shone with exhilaration that made her heart squeeze.

She had to resist the urge to fling her arms around him. She tore her eyes off his handsome face and glanced at the big black machine shining in the sun. "Is this the same bike?"

"It has a few new bits and pieces, but yes, it's the same one." He stroked a broad hand over the leather seat. Her belly tingled as if he was stroking her.

"I can't believe you got it to run after ten years."

"It wasn't easy. I've worked on nothing else all weekend. But I think it was waiting for me."

He looked up at her, his expression suddenly shy.

Her heart tripped.

He glanced behind her to the house. Panic rippled through her. "Would you like to come in?"

"Sure." He strode toward her, his confident step at odds with his wary expression.

She'd never asked him into the house when they were

kids. She'd never have dared. Her mother would have given her a tongue lashing to shred her epidermis.

But she was an adult and this was her home, too, at least when she was back in Maine.

She held the door open for him and he stooped under the low lintel. A plain white T-shirt skimmed the hard muscle of his shoulders and fell past the waistband of his jeans.

She didn't look any lower. No need to start drooling right now. He certainly did look more like the Declan she remembered, which stirred a disturbing warmth in her chest.

"Oh, goodness!" Her mother stood in the hallway with a hand pressed to her breast as if she'd just been surprised by bandits.

"Mom, have you ever met Declan Gates?" She tried to sound breezy.

"No, I don't believe I have." Her mother slid her glasses into position. She seemed to shrink backward even as she held her hand out for him to shake.

Declan stepped forward and shook it. "Pleased to meet you, Mrs. Wharton." Was that a note of triumph in his voice?

Lily slipped past Declan and led the way into the kitchen. "Would you like to come in and have a cup of tea? We were just polishing the silver." She ignored the look of alarm on her mother's face.

Declan followed her through the sitting room and into the kitchen. He looked around him like Aladdin in the magic cave. He seemed huge in the low-ceilinged room, though he probably wasn't much over six feet. The wrought iron pot hanger dangled its wares danger- ously close to his head.

"What kind of tea do you like?"

"Actually, I don't like tea." His eyes twinkled. "I came here to ask you to come to dinner with me."

Lily stared. What happened to the cold, hard Declan who threatened to destroy her dreams?

"At Luigi's?" The town only had one restaurant still operating. She could picture the entire town standing, noses pressed to the plate glass window, mouths gaping.

"At the house. I'm a pretty mean cook."

She realized her mouth was hanging open and she snapped it shut.

He was going to cook for her? She couldn't resist that. "Um, okay. Yes." Her heart raced. She should hate herself for being so easy after the way he'd treated her last time she was at the house.

Or was it she who'd been rude and demanding? She couldn't remember now, as her thoughts were scram- bled by the sight of Declan in her mother's kitchen.

By the hopeful expression in his wide, gray eyes.

"Shall we get going?"

"Um, sure, let me just…" She glanced down. Jeans and T-shirt. Fine. Was she wearing makeup? No. Oh, well. She darted out of the kitchen and into the bathroom where she checked her hair in the mirror. Her face was flushed. How embarrassing that her excitement was so obvious.

Should she grab a couple of things like…a change of underwear and her diaphragm?

No! She blew out a breath and fanned herself. How presumptuous. Besides, Declan had condoms last time.

She bit her lip to stop a wicked grin sneaking across her face. *Get a grip, Lily! Two days ago this man was threatening to sell the factory out from under you.*

She straightened her shoulders, lifted her chin and marched into the hallway.

Declan and her mom were discussing the impressive run of sunny days they'd enjoyed. What next?

"Would you put some more gas in the car for me, dear?" Her mom put a hand on her arm as she passed her in the hall.

"Lily won't be taking the car." Declan's eyes glittered.

Lily's adrenaline surged. Should she insist on taking the car so she had a means of escape? Going on his bike would put her at Declan's mercy—in more ways than one.

Her mother's fingers tightened around her arm. "Lily, you know how I feel about motorcycles."

And Declan Gates.

She tugged her arm free. "See you later, Mom." As a teen she would never have dared to openly flaunt even an unspoken rule. But she wasn't a kid anymore.

She strode to the front door without a backward glance at her mother's no-doubt horrified expression.

Excitement trickled to her fingertips as she looked at the sleek, black machine. Declan climbed aboard and gestured for her to mount behind him. With a deep breath she lifted her leg and stretched it as high as she could—then slid in behind Declan, settling onto the wide leather seat like it was a saddle.

"Put your arms around my waist."

She could see his smile, even from behind. She slid her hands over the soft cotton of his T-shirt and settled them on his flat belly. Her breasts brushed his back, making the position dangerously sensual.

"Comfy?" Declan turned his head just enough for their eyes to meet.

"Yes," she managed, pressing her palms against his waist. If he was as aroused as she was, this journey could be perilous for both of them.

He started the engine and the throaty growl shivered through her.

How many times had she dreamed of doing this? Her mother must be watching from inside the house, no doubt shaking her head and muttering with disgust, which only enhanced the girlish thrill of the occasion.

"Whoa!" She couldn't stop the cry escaping from her lips as the bike lurched into action. She tightened her arms around Declan, leaning so close that her face almost touched his neck. His own musky smell mingled with leather and metal and fuel to create a scent that was reassuring and enervating at the same time.

Ohmygosh. The bike picked up speed and Lily clung tighter. Declan's warm, solid body felt totally at ease. The wind whipped through her hair, reminding her that she should be wearing a helmet.

She should be studying those legal documents relating to her IPO that her attorney had sent her.

She should be catching up on all the sleep she'd be missing this week in the office.

She should—

"Whaaa!" The bike streaked forward in a burst of speed as it left the driveway to her house and zipped onto the main road. Her heart thundered against her ribcage as they leaned into a turn. Terror and exhilaration stung her fingers and toes.

Wow! This felt almost as good as skiing down White Heat.

By the time they arrived back at the house she'd learned to relax into sharp turns and bursts of speed, molding her body to Declan's and enjoying the thrill of motion without an accompanying tug of fear.

When he spoke she had to lean in close to reply, her lips brushing his neck and ear as she inhaled the wild, delicious smell of him along with the sharp sea air.

As they pulled up in front of the house her blood was humming and throbbing along with the engine, and it almost hurt to hear him turn it off.

He extended a hand to support her as she stepped off.

"My legs are shaking. I'm not sure they're ready for solid ground." She giggled, staggering slightly.

Declan grinned. "Solid ground is a little too dull once you've got used to riding the wind."

He lifted his leg over the bike in one smooth motion, like he'd been doing it every day for the past ten years. Watching him made her feel giddier than ever.

He stowed the bike in the carriage house, where he'd moved a stand into the center of one of the bays, between two covered cars. A mix of tools lay scattered on a tarp on the floor.

Curiosity pricked her. Or was it a sense of winning a coup? "What made you decide to fix it up?"

Declan gave her a sly look. "I think you know exactly why I did it."

"Because I told you to go look for your soul?"

A smile crept across his insolent mouth. "No one ever accused me of having a soul before."

She arched a brow. "A soul can be a dangerous thing. It can make you feel more than you want to."

The wind tossed his black hair. "Lucky thing I like to live dangerously."

Lily was certainly feeling more than she wanted to as Declan led her to the house and she stepped into the stone-and-oak splendor of the foyer. Just two days ago she'd been spitting venom at him right here.

"Do you still like the sound of my bike?" His expression, both arrogant and wary, tugged at something deep inside her.

"I *love* it. And the sound is nothing compared to the buzz of riding it. I had no idea what I'd been missing out on all these years."

"I've missed you, Lily." Declan looked her dead in the eye, his clear gaze holding nothing back. "I thought I was used to people hating me. Heck, I've had enough practice over the years that I admit I even kind of like it. When someone hates you, at least you know where you stand. I could even say that being despised is part of my pregame preparation for some business deals. Less surprises that way."

His chest expanded as he drew in a deep breath.

"But when you looked at me like that. So angry, so…
disappointed." He shook his head. "You made me look
inside myself, and what I saw wasn't pretty."

"Are you sure it wasn't your bike you looked inside
of?" She crossed her arms and tried not to smile.

"Maybe it came down to the same thing." His long
lashes shaded his eyes as his mouth tilted into a smile.
"Hey, I asked you here to eat, and I've got you
standing around listening to me bare my soul. You like
Chinese?"

"Love it."

Lily chopped broccoli and bok choy while Declan
tailed and deveined some shrimp and sprinkled them
with pepper sauce. In addition to the dinner ingredients,
he'd picked up some candles, and the interior of the vast
old kitchen glowed in the soft light.

"You've had a cleaner in, haven't you?" The place
looked spotless. The vintage cooking range and the
enormous porcelain sink shone.

"And an exterminator. The place is almost fit for
human habitation."

"It's beautiful." She rubbed the scarred pine of the
massive table that functioned as the kitchen island.

Declan's hair hung in his eyes as he whipped garlic,
scallions and ginger together with aromatic sesame oil
and soy sauce in a bowl. His tan forearms held steady
and his wrist moved in a practiced rhythmic motion
that appeared to be second nature.

He looked so…at home.

A ripple of panic swept through her. "Are you falling in love with the house?"

His head snapped up. "With this place? Hell no." He turned and tossed the mixture into the wok where it burst into a rush of sound and steam. "I guess staying here is a way for me to confront the past and shake it loose."

Declan scraped the chopped vegetables into the sizzling oil.

"To say goodbye?"

He turned and stared at her, a strange expression on his face. "Yeah. Maybe that is it. Not to say goodbye to the house, because it's just a house." He picked up the bowl of shrimp and tossed them with a fork. "But maybe I need to say goodbye to my dad. To my brothers."

He dropped the shrimp into the wok where they crackled and spat.

"You still miss them."

"I'll always miss them, but I don't want to live in the past, wondering what might have been, you know?"

He stirred the wok and steam billowed high in the air. "You've got to live in the present. Speaking of which, can you pass me the noodles?"

Their fingers touched as she handed him the colander, sparking a shimmer of awareness. He stirred the cooked noodles into the mix, then transferred the fragrant stir-fry into two large bowls.

"Wow, that smells great! How did you learn how to cook?"

"A man's gotta eat."

They carried their bowls and chopsticks into the

dining room and sat at the gleaming table with glasses of golden Chablis.

"You always could do anything you set your mind to." She peered at him over the rim of her wineglass.

"You, too." He raised a brow.

"I guess that's one thing we have in common." She took a sip of the cool liquid. "That and being as stubborn as a mule."

Declan's lips curved into a smile. "Someone once told me mules aren't stubborn, they're just smart."

"Another thing we have in common."

"Along with modesty." He winked.

"Seriously though, how many people could have predicted that we'd both be successful business owners in our twenties? How often does that happen?"

Declan shrugged. "We're hardworking and determined." He expertly lifted noodles to his mouth with the chopsticks, then chewed and swallowed. "And I'm as ruthless as hell."

"So I've read. Your name is feared on every continent." She took a bite of tasty shrimp.

"They're probably still scrawling it on bathroom walls with a string of obscenities, just like old times." A wicked grin spread across his face. "Lucky thing the Blackrock school of hard knocks grew me a thick skin."

"Life and business don't have to be a battle, you know?" Lily gathered some noodles between her chopsticks. "I've built a fifteen-million-dollar business without making a single enemy."

"I'd miss the taste of blood in my mouth after a great

deal. I enjoy a fight." He tilted his head back and looked at her through narrowed eyes. Aggressive.

But Lily wasn't scared. Declan's toughness was rooted in a strong sense of right and wrong. That's the thing no one else ever took the time to learn about him. Judging from the articles she'd read, he hadn't changed at all. He didn't care about bad press, but when she looked past the bluster and shocking headlines she could see he always did the right thing.

She was possibly the only person in the world who truly understood him.

"You might find there are more effective ways to get what you want. Gentle persuasion for example. It's rumored to work better with women." She sipped her wine to hide a smile. The question burning in her brain sprang to her lips. "How come you've never married?"

"And risk ending up like my dad? No thanks." He shot her a wry smile. "Besides, a girl I used to know spoiled me for all other women."

His thick lashes didn't quite hide a sly look.

Her heart contracted. "Stop teasing! I bet you've dated hundreds of women."

His eyes glittered in the candlelight. "Thousands, maybe." A smile played across his lips. "But none of them ever lived up to the memories I have of that one girl."

"Maybe even she wouldn't live up to your memories?" Lily took a bite of shrimp and tried to distract herself with its spicy taste. "You could hardly expect her to be the same person after all those years."

"Oh, I wouldn't want her to be." He leaned forward. "Back then she had some…hang-ups." One dark brow lifted.

"Maybe she still has them." Fear mingled with anticipation in her gut.

Declan held her gaze with his cool gray eyes. "I know one way to find out."

Eight

As soon as they'd finished their stir-fry, Declan rose and disappeared into the kitchen. He returned with an elegant silver bowl. "Follow me and bring the wine."

Frowning at his brusque command, Lily obeyed. She kept pace, trying not to spill, as he took the polished stairs two at a time. "Where are we going?"

He ignored her. He strode along the hallway, boot heels tapping on the wood floor, then pushed a door open with his hip.

"The master bedroom?" She'd redone it for the shoot. Everything had to be custom-made for the odd-sized antique furniture. She'd loved the way her heavy cream matelassé and the bold black-on-ivory engraved wallpaper had contrasted with the carved mahogany of the Victorian bed.

"If this is the master bedroom, that makes me the master, because I've been sleeping in it." He put the bowl on the heavy mahogany dresser. "So you—" he took the glasses from her hand and set them on the dresser "—must be my mistress."

His words, rasped low, shivered through her.

Her mouth fell open, surprised, wordless.

He took a step toward her and touched the bare skin of her upper arms with his palms. Heat gathered in her chest as he slid his forearms around her back, encasing her—trapping her—in his embrace.

The shocking idea of being Declan Gates's mistress—even for a single minute—should make her run screaming.

They'd already made love once. If they did it again, it was more than a fling. It was heading into the treacherous territory of an "affair."

But she didn't feel like struggling.

His face hovered inches from hers, his spicy male smell a sweet torment. She watched his mouth, serious and sensual at the same time. He studied her, those appraising gray eyes taking in every feature of her face with rapt concentration.

Then, very slowly, he lowered his lips to hers. Her mouth hummed with anticipation as he grew closer. For an instant he hovered there, an infinitesimal distance between them, as excitement gathered like a storm.

His tongue flicked once over her mouth, sparking a flash of longing, before his lips settled over hers and claimed them with a kiss.

Her hands flew to his back and she pressed her body against his. Her breasts stirred at the pleasure of being crushed against him.

They deepened their kiss, his fingers roving into her hair, his palms sweeping over her until all her skin was alive and tingling.

When their lips finally parted she gasped for air.

"So far, so good, Mistress Lily." His eyes took on a wicked gleam. "But now it's time for dessert." In a swift movement he lifted his T-shirt over his head.

She inhaled sharply at the sight of his perfectly toned torso with its line of soft black hair pointing to the fly of his jeans.

Without thinking she reached out and unbuttoned the heavy denim. Unzipped the fly and pushed his jeans down over his firm backside.

The bulge in his black boxers made her fingers tingle.

She knelt and lowered his jeans over his powerful thighs and rock-hard calves, and he stepped out.

"You must be naked." His deep voice carried the hint of a threat, which strangely heightened her excitement.

He lifted her T-shirt over her head and removed her jeans, bra and underwear with careful fingers. Arousal rippled through her in waves that made her want to laugh or shout, but she kept it all battened down, saving it, letting it build.

At last he slid off his own boxers and they stood facing each other. Desire crackled in the air between them for an instant before Declan turned and strode across the room.

"Where are you going?" Her legs shook with the intensity of her need.

He grabbed a bowl off the dresser and walked to the bed, where he sat on the thick matelassé. His tan skin glowed against the luscious creamy fabric.

"Come here."

She climbed up onto the bed, enjoying the cool soft cotton under her hot skin. She shifted until they sat side by side, her smooth thigh brushing his rough one.

Declan picked up a large strawberry and held it out. She could smell its ripe sweetness as she took a bite. The juice wet her lips and dribbled down her chin.

"This is kind of messy."

"All the better." Declan leaned forward and licked the juice off her chin. The rasp of his tongue made her skin tingle. She couldn't suppress a giggle.

Glancing down, she saw the silver bowl was filled with fresh berries. She picked up a plump blackberry and lifted it to his lips.

She loved the sensual cut of his mouth, both full and firm at the same time. Her belly quivered with desire as she watched him open it to accept the dark, shiny mouthful.

Lashes lowered, he crunched the berry between white teeth. Then he eased himself backward on the bed until he lay with his head and shoulders propped against a pillow.

Feeling naughty, she picked up a raspberry and placed it between the fullest part of her breasts. Declan climbed over her, one hand planted on either side of her hips. She wriggled slightly so her hips brushed against his wrists creating yet more electricity between them.

He gave her a hungry look, then leaned forward and lowered his mouth. Her nipples tightened in anticipation. His silky hair skimmed her skin for an instant, then his face brushed the sides of her breasts as he dove between them to take his mouthful.

His eyes shone, pupils dilated with raw lust, as he lifted his head, chewing.

She licked her lips and let a wicked smile spread across them. "Inhibitions? What are those?"

Declan's heavy-lidded stare made her arms and legs tense and shivery. His dark head moved lower, between her legs. When his tongue flicked over her sensitive flesh, fierce ripples of awareness sped to her toes, her fingers and everywhere in between.

One of them must have escaped to her brain because suddenly through the mist of sensation came a single shard of thought, piercing in its clarity.

She gripped the thick, soft coverlet with sweating hands, trying to gain a purchase in reality.

Was this seduction part of a quest for revenge?

The thought snuck across her mind like a ray of cool moonlight in the smoky darkness of her desire.

But it was no use. Her hips bucked as Declan's tongue sent another ruthless wave of longing surging through her.

She opened her eyes and saw his face buried between her legs, his thick black hair mingled with her dark gold hair.

A strange laugh ripped from her lungs and made him look up. His heavy lidded eyes met hers with a questioning glance.

She couldn't stop the laughter that bubbled up inside her. She didn't care if he wanted revenge. She wanted *him*.

She wriggled down under him, cupping his hard jaw with her hands. His own laugh, deep and throaty, mingled with hers to make music that filled the silent air of the bedroom.

His muscled chest collided with her breasts as he slid upward, his rough textured thighs rubbing over her smooth ones, his arms pulling him up until they were face-to-face, staring into each other's eyes.

"You brought me back here, Lily." His gray gaze held her still. "I wasn't ever coming back."

"You make it sound like I enchanted you."

"Maybe you did." He shifted, stirring delicious vibrations in her limbs. The pressure of his erection against her belly made her want him inside her.

"I never knew I had magical powers." She'd meant to sound dismissive, but the words emerged hushed, a whisper.

He paused and tilted his head slightly as if wanting to see her from another angle. "You do over me. You always have."

The cautious look in his eyes sparked a strange tingle under her skin. "The kind of magic that could make you bring your old bike back to life?"

He dipped his head a second and his hair brushed her

face, then he looked back up at her. "The kind of magic that could bring the old *me* back to life."

His serious expression told her he really meant it. Her heart swelled and she struggled to get control of the mass of undefined feelings roiling inside her.

"There's no denying that at least one part of you is very much alive," she quipped, raising her belly against his erection, trying to lighten the mood.

His eyes creased into a smile and his teeth gleamed. "I'm under an enchantment. What can I say? I'm helpless."

Laughter shook both their chests. There was no one on the planet less helpless than Declan Gates. A point he proved by sucking each of her nipples into hard peaks while he teased her almost to the point of madness with his deft fingertips.

He cast his own wicked spell on her, getting her so aroused she was ready to burst into flames. She writhed, unable to control the almost convulsive movements of her limbs. Surely even immolation would bring blessed relief from the torment of desire stinging every inch of her body.

She was ready to cry out in desperation when he finally entered her, sliding in with a swift precision that took her breath away.

He pressed his face to her neck and breathed kisses into her hair, enveloping her whole body in a caress that said more than words.

Tears pricked the corners of her eyes as she held him close, buried inside her. This moment was so perfect, so clear and sharp, so intense—like something that *had* to happen.

She nuzzled his hair and rubbed her nose over his cheek, reveling in the rich masculine scent of his hair and skin, as they started to move. Waves of pleasure rippled through her as he stirred inside her, his hips guiding them both deeper and deeper into their own private world.

He murmured her name—*Lily*—over and over like a mantra until they both seemed to float in a field of lilies while they held each other in the warm darkness.

Locked together, they moved so slowly that it was barely movement at all. They wanted to prolong the delicious anguish of their excitement for a few more moments, fighting the urge to move, to thrust and push and rub the raw itch of their lust. Her insides throbbed and pulsed, as their arms wrapped tighter and tighter around each other.

At last Declan broke the spell by thrusting deeper than she ever thought possible, penetrating all the way to some core of herself that she didn't even know was there.

She gave an audible cry as lights and colors exploded across her brain and her body spasmed with tremors. Declan groaned, long and low, as his own release ploughed through him with relentless force.

Shaking and breathless, they collapsed onto the soft cotton covers until the tension seeped out of them and they lay tangled together, heavy with relief.

When Declan finally opened his eyes, a single sliver of pale moonlight sliced through the thick musky darkness that enveloped the room. It skated over both their bodies, linking their entwined limbs like a skein of silver thread.

Lily slept, her soft hair splayed on the pillow, her parted lips warming his shoulder with her breath.

Declan arched his back and stretched, distorting the band of moonlight that tied him to Lily. He removed the condom, relieved that he'd had the foresight to put one on at all. Lily had the ability to deprive him of his senses.

Damn, it was worth it, though. A grin snuck across his mouth as he looked at her sleeping form. So feminine and delicate, everything about her perfect.

And he'd won her back. Like an errant knight who'd set out to court his maiden, ridden to her on his black charger, swept her back to his castle and...

Well. They probably didn't do this in the old days, at least not if they weren't married.

He tensed. Marriage? Where had that grim thought come from?

He certainly had no intention of marrying anyone. Ever. Especially not someone who'd rather be dead than bear the accursed name of Gates.

The thought almost made him laugh.

Almost, but not quite.

He touched Lily's chin gently with his thumb. She'd take her company public. He'd sell her the house and mill she wanted so much. He'd go back to Hong Kong or Singapore. Maybe he'd even buy himself a nice house somewhere. It was time to grow up and stop living in hotels.

He'd probably never see Maine again.

A hot panic seized him at the thought. Why? He hated Blackrock. He hadn't been here in a decade and hadn't wanted to.

Lily shifted, the silver thread of light rippling over her belly before it wound around his legs. A soft sigh escaped her lips.

He'd miss Lily.

The thought knocked the wind from his lungs. How could he? She'd spurned him and totally ignored him for ten damn years. Then when she'd needed something from him, she'd tugged him back here like a dog on a leash and roped him into her plans.

He pulled his legs up, instinctively moving them so the thread of moonlight wouldn't tie him to Lily. It sketched a bright line across the empty covers next to her sleeping body.

Much better.

He'd come here to get Blackrock, Lily and the rest of them out of his system. To face the past head-on and end its power over him. The house he'd despised was now a perfectly pleasant dwelling that Lily would no doubt enjoy spending the rest of her life in. She'd...

His blood froze at the ghastly image of Lily marrying someone. Having children with him.

No.

He flew off the bed. Tried to shake the bitter thoughts from his mind.

"Declan, where are you going?" Her sleepy voice snuck right to his heart.

"Just stretching." He turned to look at her and

warmth replaced the icy tension of a moment ago. She rolled and stretched herself, and in seconds he was back on the bed with her, skin warm against hers, kissing her awake with passion that spilled up from somewhere deep inside him. He couldn't stop himself.

"Declan, are you okay?" She gasped for air. "You seem very…intense."

"I'm fine," he muttered gruffly. That silver thread of moonlight had thickened into a rope. It now linked them both at the waist—tying them firmly together. He mirrored it with his arm, holding her tight.

"I don't think I've ever slept so well in my life. I feel so relaxed, like I could just lie here forever." Her voice sounded like music rippling through the dark, the silvery notes mingling with the first anticipatory chirps of songbirds in the trees outside.

"It must be morning." She rocketed up in bed, knocking his arm almost off her. "It's *Monday* morning!"

"Yes?" He looked at her, amused.

"Don't you have work to do?" She pressed a hand to her mouth, looking shocked.

"Nothing that can't wait," he lied.

She blew out a burst of laughter. "I'm supposed to meet with the lawyer who's writing my IPO charter this afternoon. It's almost ready."

"I know."

"You do?" She stared at him, her gaze sharp.

"Sure, I'm a financier. Following companies is my job."

"Following *my* company?"

"Of course. We have a business…entanglement." He

raised an eyebrow. "The success of your IPO affects whether you'll be able to take this old heap off my hands."

Lily narrowed her eyes. "It's going very well, you know. We've had a lot of investor interest."

"I know." A cool finger of concern touched him. "You are protected, aren't you?"

She frowned. "Protected?"

"Against people…" He licked his lips. "People like me."

Suddenly tense, he stretched. "You don't want to risk losing control of your company when you go public."

She looked at him for a moment, then humor sparkled in her eyes. "My lawyer has built a barrage of anti-takeover measures into my IPO charter."

"Good." His stomach relaxed. Of course, anti-takeover measures made it more difficult to take control of a company, but they couldn't prevent a truly determined investor. Like the kind he'd be if he'd intended to stick with his original plan.

"Speaking of protection." Lily slid off the bed and stretched, sunbeams jumping around her nude body. Declan resisted the urge to groan with desire. "Would you be so kind as to bring one of those condoms downstairs with you?"

She turned, beaming a polite smile, as if she'd asked him to carry her parasol.

"I'd be delighted." His voice emerged kind of rough. His eyes tracked her as she glided across the room and slid prim white cotton briefs on over her long elegant legs and a modest white bra over her proud, high breasts.

By the time she was done he was as hard as the mahogany bedpost.

"Breakfast time." She tossed her soft blond hair and disappeared out the door, wearing nothing but her underwear.

Fighting the urge to pant, Declan prowled right behind her, the condom packet burning in his hand as excitement and curiosity seethed in his body.

"Would you look at the sunrise through this window?" Lily stood at the top of the stairs. Sunlight filled the long window that lit the stairwell, flashing jewel tones on the sparkling antique glass.

"What sunrise?" Declan couldn't tear his eyes from Lily's scantily clad body. He walked toward her and slid his arm around her waist. Naked himself, he pressed his solid erection against her snowy cotton briefs.

The thick wooden banister curved below them. "I used to slide down this banister," he whispered in her ear. "It's quite a rush."

From behind, he watched her smile tighten the skin over her cheekbones. "It is unusually wide, isn't it."

The smooth polished wood swept around the wide staircase in an unbroken arc. A remembered flash of excitement shimmered through him at the memory of that wild ride.

"No knobs, either. My brothers and I used to wonder if it was made to slide on. Those crazy Whartons who designed it—who knows what they were thinking?" He ran his fingers over her belly, which tightened under his touch.

"I must have inherited my wild side from some-where." She splayed her long fingers over the wide banister. She flashed a smile at him. "You already know I can't say no to a dare."

"Go on, then." With some reluctance he released her warm body and crossed his arms over his chest. He grew harder by the second as Lily raised her hips and eased her firm butt onto the shiny wood.

"Wait." He jumped down the stairs and positioned himself at the bottom. His arms tingled with the desire to catch her in midair. "Do you trust me to catch you? Because you can go a lot faster if you don't have to land on your feet at the end."

Lily's lips parted. Then she pressed them together. Her eyes gleamed with determination.

She adjusted her seat and got herself into position, both legs pointed toward the stairs. She rocked a little, finding her center of gravity, then launched herself into a sidesaddle slide.

Declan felt his face split into a huge grin as she stuck her arms out to the side and picked up speed, leaning into the single turn. He braced himself as she shot to-ward him, hair flying out, eyes wide.

She almost knocked the breath from his lungs as she pitched off the end of the rail and slammed into him. He fell back and rolled, his arms tight around her, absorb-ing the impact as they hit the hardwood floor.

Laughter peeled out of both of them.

"Wow! Are you okay? Did that hurt?" She stared at him once they'd stopped moving.

"I don't feel a thing," he rasped. He buried his face in her neck. "But I think I lost the condom."

"You'd better find it, and quick."

Her hands slid over his skin, sparking a fierce rush of arousal. Her teeth grazed his jaw as she climbed over him, still panting with exhilaration, and kissed him hard on the mouth.

"Is that what you call *gentle persuasion?*" Urgency sent extrasensory powers shooting along his nerve endings, and within microseconds he located the lost condom packet beneath his left elbow. "I got it."

"Thank God," she gasped, as she trailed a line of kisses along his chest. He struggled with the packet as Lily tormented him almost to insanity with subtle gyrations of her hips.

"Let me help you," she murmured, polite even in this moment of near crisis. With fingers defter than his, she tore it open, then pulled back and slid it on over his throbbing flesh.

He groaned with pleasure. The wood floor felt like a bed of petals as she took him inside her, warm and wet, her virginal white underwear pushed to the side.

He skated a thumb over her white bra and her nipple grew hard. She arched her back, taking him deeper, until he could barely contain himself.

She trusted me to catch her.

His heart swelled. She'd shown no doubt that she'd believed in him, like she did all those years ago when she'd chosen to be friends with him against the advice of everyone she knew.

"Kiss me, Declan." Her breath heated his lips just before they met hers. He crushed her to him, arms tight around her slender ribcage, unable to restrain himself from seizing control of their rhythmic movement.

Sunlight from the bright window danced over his closed eyelids, making his inner world glow blood red. A sensation of piercing bliss stung him, the joy too intense to be entirely comfortable. He felt more alive than he had in years—so aroused he could hardly stand it, his heart so full—

He gasped as she rocked back, pulling him tighter and deeper inside her. He gripped her arms trying to keep from losing control.

But he couldn't stop the inevitable. He exploded inside her just as Lily cried out his name. Her voice rang off the walls, the window, the grand staircase, brimming with emotion that echoed deep inside him.

I love her.

The thought shot through him with the thunderbolt of his release. He couldn't help it any more than he could help breathing.

But the aftertaste of those words stung like deadly poison.

Nine

Lily was still flushed and tingling from head to toe by the time they arrived back at her mother's house. It was nearly noon and she had no intention of explaining what they'd done in the intervening hours.

Since their breathless encounter at the foot of the stairs, Declan had been silent, maybe stunned, as she was, by the intensity of what had happened between them.

She shook her head as she remembered sliding down the banister. Only Declan could even come up with the idea for something that imprudent—and only she would be lunatic enough to actually do it!

"What are you laughing at?" Declan turned to her after shutting off the engine.

"You, me…both of us."

A strange expression darkened his eyes. "What do you mean?"

That we're soulmates.

"Oh, nothing. Just that we're both crazy when you scratch off the thin veneer of civilization."

Relief softened his hard expression.

Why couldn't she tell him the truth? Because unspoken boundaries still hummed between them? Ramparts manned by the ghost of the Gates/Wharton feud?

Or maybe she just didn't want to scare him off. Life had taught her to smooth her path with feminine wiles rather than brutal honesty.

For once she'd like to fling aside tact and good taste and even good sense and tell him exactly how she felt. That she'd fallen in love with him, just like she always knew she would if she allowed herself to stray in his direction.

Declan held his hand steady to support her as she climbed off his bike. Her legs were still shaky, as much from their bone-shattering lovemaking as from the wind-blown ride back from the house.

Maybe she had told him how she felt. If not with her words, she'd told him with her body, with her heart.

He didn't dismount. "I'd better get going."

"Sure." She ran a hand through her tangled hair, hoping her disappointment didn't show on her face. "Thanks for dinner."

His eyes sparkled. "Thank *you.*"

Silence vibrated between them for a moment, pierced only by the plaintive wail of a gull. "Will you be staying in the house?" Her words tumbled out of her mouth, too urgent, too desperate.

"No. I have to go to Singapore for a series of meetings. I'll be gone for a while. I hope everything goes smoothly with the IPO."

"You'll probably know before I do if it doesn't." She smiled. Somehow the idea of Declan keeping track of her unfolding business gave her a sense of protection rather than anxiety.

She trusted him. The way he'd caught her at the bottom of the stairs, taken the full brunt of the impact and absorbed it for both of them in his hard muscle, still made her heart squeeze. He'd done it to prove something to her—and he'd proved it.

"Take care, Declan." She leaned forward to kiss him.

Her skin tingled as their lips touched. Then he drew back, started the ignition and left without a backward glance.

She stood at the top of the drive, the sound of his bike engine vibrating through her along with all the powerful new emotions he'd awakened.

"Goodness gracious! I was about to start calling the local emergency rooms." Her mother's voice startled Lily out of her trance.

"I spent the night at Declan's." Her voice sounded wistful, as though she were still half dreaming.

"In that house?" Her mother's horrified stare seemed to have no effect on her.

"Yes, it's very comfortable since we fixed it up for the Macy's shoot. Declan's been staying there."

Her mother raised a slim eyebrow. "So he means to keep it? Is he going to sell the factory to Textilecom?"

"You know," Lily fought a smile. "We actually didn't talk about that at all. But he'll sell them to me, I know he will."

I trust him.

She hugged herself, suddenly chilly in the morning breeze. She was still wearing yesterday's T-shirt, crumpled from spending the night on the floor.

"I suppose it would have been dangerous to ride that nasty machine back in the dark. And it is a big house." Her mother pressed her lips together. "With lots of rooms."

Yes, Mom, I slept with him. Again, she fought a smile.

"Goodness, Lily, if I didn't know you better I'd be worried that you did suffer a concussion. What are you thinking riding right through town where anyone could see you with that man?"

Anger snapped Lily out of her reverie. "Declan Gates survived a horrible childhood—made worse by the cruelty he experienced at the hands of the people in this town, including myself. He's not only survived, but he's become a great success. I'm proud to be seen with him."

Pride burned inside her and sent blood rushing to her face.

"But you read those articles. He's ruthless, without scruples!" Her mother pulled her thin sweater around herself.

"No, he isn't. He has his own code of honor. You just

have to read between the lines to see it because he doesn't feel the need to apologize or explain to anyone."

"Well, well, well. If I didn't know better…" Her mother's mouth twisted.

Lily affected a polite smile. "Tea?"

Lily's meeting with the lawyers went smoothly. Everything was in place for the initial public offering of Home Designs, Inc. on the New York Stock Exchange on the last day of August. Only three weeks away.

She hadn't heard a word from Declan, but somehow a thin thread of hope connected her to him, all those miles away in Singapore.

There were no promises between them, not even any tacit understandings, just a deep connection she'd tried to sever, but had never truly been able to.

Where it might lead was anyone's guess but that wasn't something she should think about right now. She needed to focus all her energy on guiding her young, growing company safely through the IPO and into what she anticipated would be an explosive period of growth.

The new Macy's collections were hitting stores in September, and a barrage of print ads were going into magazines and newspapers across the country, gaining her company national recognition.

She didn't have time to worry about what might—or might not—happen between her and Declan Gates.

Until her period failed to show up.

It was after 7:00 p.m. and nearly everyone had left the Home Designs offices—located in a pretty Boston brownstone—except Lily, who couldn't quite bring herself to go home alone.

She felt safer in her spacious, well-lit office, surrounded by her familiar computers and swatches and motivational posters.

The stick with its pink handle and cheery ++ sat in the drawer in front of her, hidden in an envelope. She could almost hear it throbbing like the tell-tale heart in Edgar Allen Poe's story.

Or maybe it was her heart making all that racket.

She punched in the number to dial her sister, and almost immediately Katie's merry "Helloooo" assaulted her through her cell phone.

"It's Lily." She hesitated, pressing the slim phone to her ear. Her sister was not the world's greatest keeper of secrets. The sound of Katie's one-year-old twins' yelling in the background ratcheted her blood pressure up another notch.

"One moment… Tommy, put that down! You can't eat cat food."

Lily pressed a damp palm to her forehead.

"Sorry, Lily, I swear, I was so worried about them being delayed crawlers because of their premature delivery. What was I thinking? They're into everything." Her sister's happiness shone in her voice.

Lily swallowed.

"So how are things? You must be going crazy getting everything ready for the IPO. I'm going crazy trying to keep from switching back to disposable diapers. I know the cloth ones are supposed to be better for the environment, but the service only comes once a week and that smell could—"

"Katie, I'm pregnant." Lily blurted it out, knowing her sister was quite capable of carrying on a one-sided conversation for thirty minutes.

"I told Harry I don't mind the extra work it's the... *What?*"

"I'm pregnant." The whispered words echoed off the oak expanse of her antique desk.

"You mean, with a baby?"

Her sister's raw incredulity forced a laugh to her dry throat. "No, with a space alien! Of course it's a baby."

A baby. Right there. Right now. Underneath the fitted waistband of her perfectly respectable gray-and-white houndstooth Lands' End suit.

She sucked in a deep breath as that strange mix of joy and terror snuck over her again.

"You didn't mention anyone at the barbeque last week." Her sister's bubbly voice had turned quiet. "Who are you seeing?"

Lily stood up from her chair and shoved a hand through her hair. "Declan Gates."

There was a pause so long and silent she began to wonder if the call was dropped.

"You mean, *the* Declan Gates? Of *those* Gateses? The one with the red snake tattooed on his forearm?"

Lily closed her eyes. "Declan doesn't have a tattoo. That was his older brother, Ronnie, but otherwise, yes."

"Oh my God." Her horrified silence pulsed in the air.

"I'm beginning to regret calling you for support."

Lily walked to the window and peered out at the street. People were going about their business on the sidewalk below as if this were a perfectly ordinary day.

"I'm sorry I'm just…gobsmacked. Are you okay?"

"Yes, strangely enough I'm fine. Pregnancy is a perfectly normal thing that happens to people all the time." Katie's appalled reaction seemed to put things in perspective. It wasn't like the damn world was ending!

"Not to me. I needed three rounds of IVF. When did you sleep with Declan Gates?"

"A couple of weeks ago. And a couple of weeks before that. I must have gotten pregnant the first time, because I've missed a period already." She'd been so busy she hadn't noticed until her monthly grocery delivery had shown up with the usual new box of tampons in it—and she realized she hadn't opened the box from last month.

"So what are you going to, you know, do?" Katie's voice sounded tremulous. She'd tried so hard to have her own babies, one reason Lily knew this pregnancy—

unplanned as it was—was a gift.

"I'm going to raise her to be a tough cookie like her mom."

Katie's laugh burst out of the phone. "You're so calm! I can't believe it. I'd be a basket case. But then you are a tough cookie, aren't you?"

"I'd better be. At least business is going well, so I know the baby and I will be fine for money."

"What about…Declan." She sounded as if she could

hardly spit out the name. "How on earth did it happen? Did you sleep with him so he'd sell you the house and mill?"

"Katie! Of course not. I slept with him because…" Her ribcage tightened over her heart.

Because I love him.

"I don't know. It just happened."

"Is this my sensible baby sister, Lily, or has *she* been abducted by aliens?"

"Katie! This is serious."

"Tell me about it. Have you told him?"

"Not yet. I can't tell him something like this over the phone and he's in Singapore until the end of the month. I'd rather wait until after the IPO to tell him, anyway. I'm so busy and stressed I really don't need another thing to worry about right now."

"Good idea to wait. One in four pregnancies end in miscarriage before the twelfth week."

Katie's soft words struck her like a blow. Her sister had suffered two miscarriages before conceiving her twins. "I'm going to be careful. I know it sounds strange but I'm ready for this. Maybe it's being around your babies or something, but I can't wait to have my own."

"You are scaring the heck out of me, Lily Wharton! Have you been drinking the Gates moonshine or something?"

Lily cleared her throat. "It was just one sip and that had nothing to do with anything."

"You always did have a thing for Declan Gates, didn't you? Now that I think about it you were pretty quick to defend him against nasty gossip when we were in school. Remember that time everyone was whispering about how he seduced a girl and got her pregnant?"

How could I forget. I started it.

Lily took a deep breath. "Well, now it's true."

"Wow. Mom will be fit to be tied."

"Yes." Anxiety churned in her belly. "Mind keeping quiet about it for a while? I do want Declan to be the first to know. After you, of course. I had to tell someone or I'd go right out of my mind." She glanced down at the people on the street below.

Her fingers grew cold. "Also, news that I'm pregnant could affect my IPO. You know how people get about women in business and the dreaded mommy track."

"Good point. I'll seal my lips with Super Glue. Maybe that way I'll finally lose some of the pregnancy weight."

Lily chuckled. "Okay, maybe I am glad I called you. You always remind me the world doesn't revolve around me."

"Of course! Because it revolves around me. Love you!"

Lily shook her head and ended the call.

She couldn't help smiling as she rested her hand on the still flat expanse of her belly. Inside her the two sets of warring genes—Wharton and Gates—were fusing together to create a new person. A stark transformation from the decades of anger and resentment that had made open friendship between her and Declan impossible years ago.

Proof that things could change.

What would Declan think? When the question sneaked into her mind—accompanied by an attack of stomach butterflies—she reminded herself she wasn't the type of person to waste time and energy on idle speculation.

When the time came she'd tell him, and whatever his reaction was, she'd take it in stride. Until then she had a company to run and an initial public offering to prepare for.

All the more important now since she had a child to support.

Ten

"Today's the day!" Lily spoke to her reflection in the mirror as she checked her teeth for poppy seeds left over from her breakfast bagel. All clear.

Her cheeks were certainly flushed—with excitement, or nerves, or possibly the fabled glow of pregnancy.

"Come on, Lily! The opening bell waits for no one!" her assistant, Rebecca, called through the door.

Her key staff had traveled to Manhattan with her to attend the opening of the New York Stock Exchange, where—as the owner of a company going public for the first time—she'd been offered the honor of ringing the bell to start the day's trading.

"Coming."

"You look smashing!" Rebecca's red curls bounced

as she stepped out of the doorway. "Which is lucky as people will be watching you all over the world."

"Thanks. I'm about to explode with excitement." They shared a smile as they dashed toward the trading floor.

I wonder if Declan's watching.

The thought crept into her mind as she took a deep breath and stepped out onto the noisy stock-exchange floor amid the sea of blue computer screens and the crush of brokers getting ready for the trading day.

She hadn't called him even once. She'd thought about it many times, but how could she call to say hi and not mention the pregnancy?

So it was easier not to call at all.

And he hadn't called her, either.

Yes. It hurt. Every time the phone rang she literally thought "It's him." And it never was.

They didn't have any kind of formal—or even informal—relationship for her to wonder if it was over. The thought made her chest tighten.

Today after the IPO she'd let him know that she had the money he wanted. What would happen after that?

Excitement rippled through her as she climbed the steps to the raised platform where she'd ring the bell.

"Lily Wharton, this is John Thain, CEO of the New York Stock Exchange."

She plastered on a big smile. "So pleased to meet you. This is such an honor."

The last Wharton to walk onto the stock-exchange floor was probably her great grandfather Merriwether Wharton, who jumped out his office window after losing the family fortune in one week during the crash of 1929.

Things were looking up financially for the Whartons for the first time since then.

At exactly nine o'clock she pushed the button that rang the famed bell. It echoed in her blood as she held it steady, and the sound boomed out over the hushed trading floor and across the world.

Her CFO, Dave, leaned in and whispered in her ear, "Let the madness begin."

She exchanged the customary handshakes with everyone on the platform, relieved it was finally underway.

Dave was already keeping track of early figures as they descended the stairs back to the floor. Up two points already! Excitement tickled her chest.

She managed to sound reasonably coherent in an interview with a CNBC reporter, then watched on monitors—palms sweating—as the stock spiked, then leveled off a bit. Every movement in the green—or red, or blue, depending on what monitor she watched— seemed to spark a corresponding jag in her blood pressure. It was frightening and exhilarating to see her fortunes rising and falling with the whims of buyers sitting at the ends of telephones all over the world.

The morning sped by and the market capitalization of her company climbed past the thirty-five-million mark. At eleven o'clock she placed a block of her own personally held shares up for sale. Three million dollars worth. Enough to raise the money for the house.

The mill would be purchased with capital raised by the company as a whole, but the house was to be her personal property.

Hers. To decorate, live in and cherish exactly as she wanted.

The future she'd planned for Home Designs and her beloved Blackrock was on the brink of coming true.

Declan leaned forward in his chair. The afternoon sun created glare that made it hard to read his computer screens. And he was paying particular attention to the screen on the far right.

The one tracking the movement of Home Designs Inc.

"Buy another ten thousand," he murmured into his phone. "And another ten if it goes below twenty-one."

He wanted to keep the price supported at twenty-one dollars.

He leaned back and stretched his neck. He wasn't doing it out of any sappy altruism. Far too hardheaded and coldhearted for that. No, he was simply concerned with the value of *his* stake in the company.

He didn't know wallpaper and curtains, but he'd spent quality time with Lily's prospectus. Home Designs' financials were in great shape and the company's strategy promised fast yet steady growth. Added to that, he knew Lily and anything involving her was bound to be an excellent long-term investment.

He smiled as the price bumped up half a point and held steady.

Then it bumped up another half point. And a full point. Then two more points.

He brought the phone to his mouth. "What's going on?"

Down on the stock-exchange floor, Tony muttered something inaudible to someone, then spoke into the phone. "Textilecom's buying up fifty thousand shares."

Declan sat up. "Is this their first purchase?"

The roar of activity on the floor drowned out the conversation at the other end. "They've been buying since the open. They're up to almost an eleven percent stake."

Declan flew out of his chair. "Buy more. Whatever you can get. I don't want Textilecom to get a large holding."

"But the price just hit twenty-four and a quarter."

"I don't care. Buy. And keep buying."

Shit!

He strode to the window. How could he have been blind enough to let Textilecom get such a big stake? He knew they had their eye on Lily's company. Taking over Home Designs—already associated with high quality and design—was probably cheaper and easier than upgrading their own products.

Her company's growth had exploded over the last year, and its placement in Macy's was bound to generate huge sales in the near future. Why wouldn't Textilecom want to own a large piece of such a juicy pie?

He'd read Lily's IPO charter, and while she had some antitakeover measures built in—staggered board elections, for example—he knew from firsthand experience that they merely slowed the process of taking over a company.

He knew Home Designs had floated a forty-nine percent stake of the company in the IPO, but Lily couldn't buy the house with that. The house was a private purchase. She'd have to sell her personal stock to raise money for that.

Which would take her stake below fifty percent. And leave the company wide-open.

His heart pounded. There was no way he, Declan Gates, would let a third-rate rag shop like Textilecom take over Lily's company.

"What's our exposure?" he murmured into the phone.

"Eight million and climbing. Want to stop?"

"No. Keep going. What's Textilecom doing?"

"Held until twenty-seven, then started to sell."

Hah. He shoved a hand through his hair as a smile crept across his face. He'd goaded them into some profit-taking. They probably planned to buy it back when the price dropped.

"Keep buying until the close." That would fix Textilecom's wagon.

"Regardless of price?"

It took a lot to surprise Tony, but apparently Declan had succeeded today.

"You heard me."

"You're on."

The closing bell rang, signaling the end of the trading day.

"Forty-two dollars per share as the closing price! I can hardly believe it." Lily pressed a hand to her hot forehead. The whirlwind day had left her company with a market capitalization of sixty-three million dollars. More than she had ever dreamed.

If she'd known the price would rise that high she'd have waited until the afternoon to sell the shares to buy the house!

But never mind that. She had the money to buy out Declan.

Home Designs would refit the factory exactly how she wanted it, and the company could grow in any possible direction. Everything was working out exactly as she'd hoped.

No, better.

"Trading activity was pretty fevered this afternoon. Home Designs is a hot property. Don't tell me you're surprised?" Her broker was in a jovial mood.

"No, of course not." She grinned. "It just seems too good to be true."

"Lily, Joe, something a little strange." Dave, the Home Designs CFO, approached Lily and her broker with a sheaf of papers in his hand. "Apparently a lot of today's acquisitions are by a single party."

Lily froze. "Textilecom. But the antitakeover measures in the charter—surely they make an acquisition too slow and expensive?" Her pulse pounded at her temples.

"It's not Textilecom." Dave flipped through several sheets of paper. "The acquisitions are by five different holding companies…" He flipped some more.

"Yes?" Lily could hardly breathe.

"All controlled by Declan Gates."

The last wisp of air slipped from Lily's lungs. She

stared at her CFO, who'd tactfully turned back to flipping through the pages.

"How much did he buy?" Her voice sounded steady. Perhaps he wanted to bolster her success. It was in Declan's interest that she get a good price for her shares.

Dave cleared his throat. "Fifty-one percent."

Her mouth dropped open. Everything went silent. The bustle of the trading floor, the people yammering on phones, her employees gathered in celebration, all fell away, leaving a horrible yawning emptiness.

Declan had bought a majority of the stock.

Enough to *control* her company.

The sound burst back in a deafening roar.

"Didn't you see this happening?"

"I'm afraid not." Dave looked sheepish. "He bought in small blocks, and, as I said, the stocks were purchased in five different names."

"Deliberate deception," she said, mostly to herself.

"Isn't Declan Gates a friend of yours?"

"*Friend* is not the word I'd use." She'd like to find him and...

She *had* to find him. And right now. "Rebecca, can you get his office on the phone."

"His floor man is down there somewhere. He probably has him on the phone."

"Find him."

Lily paced back and forth in her broker's office, her mind jumping between the horrifying possibilities of what Declan meant to do with her company, and the even more gruesome possibilities of what she intended to do with him if she could get her hands on him.

Rebecca poked her head in. "Declan's in New York. At his office in the World Financial Center."

"You're kidding?" Lily glanced out the window. The towers of the World Financial Center shimmered in the late afternoon sun. "What's the number? I'm going over."

She grabbed her purse and briefcase off the floor.

"Building Four," said Rebecca, looking nervous. "The twenty-ninth floor. Would you like me to come, too?"

"I appreciate your willingness to follow me into battle, but I need to see him *alone*." The last word rang with menace. "Though you might want to find the number of a good trial lawyer who can defend me against a charge of grievous bodily harm."

Rebecca bit her lip and stood aside as Lily swept out the door. Her CFO and the underwriters had already made themselves scarce with supposedly urgent business. Not that they could have done anything even if they had spotted Declan swooping down like a hunting raptor.

It was a free market after all, as Dave had said, a bead of sweat quivering on his upper lip.

Lily announced herself to the security guard at reception in a clear, ringing voice. He called up to Declan's office and she heard him announce her name.

Would Declan see her? Did he *dare?* Her fingers tightened around the handle of her briefcase.

"Go right up."

Her heart thundered like a feudal war drum as she marched across the marble lobby.

The ride in the elevator seemed to take forever, and not nearly long enough. Blood pounded in her brain as she tried to think of the right words to express her sheer fury, her sense of outrage…

Of betrayal.

The doors slid open and she stepped out into the carpeted hallway and strode along the row of closed doors. The plaque next to the number she'd been given said Magnet Holdings. No doubt one of the respectable corporate fronts Declan used to perpetrate his slash-and-burn techniques on innocent corporations.

She tried the handle, but it was locked. Irritation rippled through her. She raised her fist to knock, and at that moment the handle turned and the door opened.

Declan stood there in a white shirt and dark pants, his tie loosened. His expression was serious, intense. "Hello, Lily."

She'd shouted angry speeches in her mind all the way from the NYSE, but her indignant words fled at the sight of him. His silver eyes had been filled with smiles last time they met. Echoes of the laughs they'd shared filled her chest with choking sorrow.

"Come in." He stepped aside and tore his eyes from her face with what appeared to be an effort. Emotion crackled in the air between them like static.

She followed him into a large corner office with a view out over the Hudson River. Pages spewed from a printer in one corner and monitors flashed a changing display of colored figures.

No one else around.

"Congratulations, Lily." His eyes shone.

"On what?" The words flew from her mouth.

"The success of your IPO, of course." He turned to her, smiling. He'd pulled a bottle of champagne from a small fridge.

"You're kidding, right?" Her voice was cold.

He frowned. A muscle moved in his cheek. "You closed at forty-two dollars per share. You're a rich woman."

"You think I care about that?" She blew out an exasperated breath. "I know what you did, Declan. You bought my company out from under me."

A line appeared between his brows. "I invested in you."

A sound that was half gasp, half laugh escaped her mouth. "Invested? You *bought* me. Fifty-one percent? Don't tell me that's some kind of cute coincidence. It wasn't enough for you to have a stake." Her chest heaved. "No, you had to own more than half of my company."

Tears shimmered in her voice and she tried to shove them back down. "Why, Declan? If you wanted revenge you already had it. You made love to me, you...you..."

You made me fall in love with you all over again.

She crushed the thought back into her heart. "You made me trust you. I did trust you. And now you do this? Was this the grand plan you had in mind all along?"

Declan stared at her, like she'd truly surprised him. "I bought your stock to help you."

"To help relieve me of ownership of my company? Oh, thank you very much." She hated the venom in her voice, the fear in her heart. "What next? Are you going to kick me out?"

"No." His expression darkened and he put the unopened champagne bottle down on his cluttered desk. Harsh afternoon sunlight cut bright slashes of light across the room.

He stared at her so hard she had to fight to keep steady. "Textilecom was buying up your stock. They'd made a clear move to gain control, so I stepped in to prevent them. In the trade we call it a White Knight maneuver." He blinked, his expression wary. Sunlight glittered in his silver eyes and she fought off a shimmer of emotion.

She was *not* going to be seduced by him again.

"White Knight? You mean, charging in to the rescue with your trampling armies and taking over my company yourself?"

"I don't want to take over your company." Sunlight glazed his jaw. He moved around the desk toward her. As if he wanted to touch her.

She flinched back. Resisted the appeal of his fierce gaze. "No, you just want to *own* it. To own *me*. You call yourself a White Knight." A sob colored her voice. "Well, I've seen you in action with a sword and I know exactly what kind of knight you are, Declan Gates."

He hesitated, obviously confused. Then realization dawned. "That was a fencing foil. It's just a game."

Heat burned in her chest. "It's all a game to you. This company is my life. I've worked day and night for years to build it into the modest success it is today." Her voice rose as emotion started to get the better of her. "I've dreamed and planned and slaved to get my business to the point where I could bring it home to Blackrock and save the town before it's too late."

He shoved a hand through his hair. Confusion shadowed his features. "I know. That's why I couldn't let Textilecom buy you out."

She blew out a disgusted breath. "I don't believe Textilecom had any intention of taking over Home Designs. I don't believe they wanted to buy the factory, either. I now suspect that story was manufactured by *you* to set up this whole charade. And even if you really did want to save my company from Textilecom, why did you have to buy more than half the company?" She pinned him with a stare.

Anger and hurt made it hard to talk. The words caught in her throat and she had to force them out. "Because you could, that's why. Because you have to fight and you have to win. That's what it's all about for you, isn't it?"

Declan's expression darkened. His lips parted but no sound came out.

"You had to win at all costs." She gasped for air. "You knew I'd hate it but you didn't care, you went ahead and took it, just like you take everything else you want."

Including me.

And our baby. The thought crashed inside her head like a clash of cymbals. She'd been so wound up in her IPO all day she'd barely thought about the tiny life growing inside her.

For weeks now she'd waited to tell Declan, wondered and hoped and worried about how he'd react. Now she was here, in the same room with him.

Guilt spiked inside her and tangled with her fury.

I have to go.

She couldn't stay there and not tell him, but she couldn't tell him now, not when he'd demonstrated his power over her in the crudest possible way.

She clutched her heavy briefcase to her chest like a shield. "I said you once had a soul. I thought that maybe, just maybe you'd managed to find a piece of it and bring it back to life." A rush of adrenaline streaked through her as she remembered the thrilling ride they'd shared on his motorcycle. Her hugging him, his guiding them as they whipped around corners, racing the wind.

Tears sprang to her eyes. "But I was wrong. Yes, I once treated you cruelly, I hurt you and I regret that. But I was a child, I was afraid and I wasn't in control of my own life."

She sucked in a shuddering breath. "You didn't have to pay any attention to my IPO at all. I didn't ask for your help. But you had to. You had me where you wanted me—owing you a huge sum of money—and once you got me vulnerable you pounced and sank your teeth into me."

Two hot tears rolled down her cheeks. "You're not a child with someone telling you what to do. You're a man, you make your own decisions. And you decided—in cold blood and after seducing me—to steal my company."

And I won't let you take my baby.

She took a step back, toward the door. "Yes, I have enough money to pay you for the house and the mill, but you have the power to steal them all back again and do what you want with them. When you told me you wanted them to fall into the sea I didn't believe you. But now I do."

Declan had looked stunned the whole time she was speaking. He shoved a hand through his black hair.

"Lily, you don't understand." The intense expression in his eyes called out to her as he stepped toward her. His musky scent—a painful memory of their intimacy—assaulted her as he came too close.

She stepped back again. She couldn't let him get hold of her. Even the touch of his hand might make her weaken and fall for him all over again. She had to stay strong.

Suddenly desperate to get away from the magnetic pull he had over her, she fled for the door, fighting back more tears.

"Wait!" He grabbed her arm and his fingers closed around it. She fought him for a second time, struggling like a mouse in a trap. Panic rose in her chest—he was stronger than her.

Their eyes met. The determination in his silver gaze changed to something else—shock—and his fingers loosened.

She ripped her arm from his grasp and flew out of his office.

He didn't follow her as she slammed out into the hallway and ran for the elevator, her heavy briefcase banging against her legs and her breath coming in shaky gulps.

He'd seduced her, tricked her into loving him, then stolen her company.

The printed words designed to protect her company from hostile takeover had been engineered to keep out investors motivated by business. They made it expensive and time-consuming to seize control of her company.

But they couldn't possibly keep out someone with a motive as ruthless and illogical as *revenge*.

The elevator door slid open and she jumped inside. Two white-haired businessmen stared at her tear-streaked face, but she held her shoulders high.

Any further communication with Declan Gates would be through lawyers.

A sob racked her body. How could something that seemed so beautiful, so powerful, come to this?

All those pathetic dreams that had snuck around the edge of her brain—raising their baby together, living in the house and growing old together.

What a joke. When it came to Declan Gates she should have listened to her mother's advice: stay away.

Dangerous Declan, they'd called him. Too wild, too intense, too strikingly handsome to be safe.

He seduced a girl and got her pregnant.

She'd been afraid it would happen to her. That teen-aged kiss had lit a hot spark deep inside her. Who knows what might have happened if she'd allowed it to grow into a flame when she was still young?

But she'd been more sensible then. She'd known to steer clear of forces beyond her grasp, things she didn't understand and couldn't control.

A harsh laugh mingled with a sob as she pushed out into the street and the roar of traffic filled her ears.

Live and learn, they said. Well, she had now. And she certainly wouldn't trust herself anywhere near Declan Gates ever again.

Eleven

Declan stood staring at the tall door she'd slammed in his face. Sweat dampened his skin and his muscles stung with adrenaline. Every nerve ending jumped and crackled with the urge to run after her, to chase her and grab her and hold her until he could explain.

Explain what? That she was right?

He turned and blew out a blast of air.

Light from the sun setting behind the Statue of Liberty stung his eyes. Why *had* he done it?

When Tony had told him Textilecom had bought some of Lily's stock, he'd gone into full-fledged battle mode, as she so colorfully described.

Almost like he'd just been waiting for an excuse.

He paced back and forth in his office. A phone rang and he ignored it.

Buying up all that stock had felt good. Right.

Being a White Knight rushing to the defense of his fair maiden felt even better.

And owning more than half Lily's company?

Guilt and shame pierced him like an enemy lance.

She was right. He had to win. It was how he played the game. Once he threw his hat into the ring, no one was leaving until he waved his bloody sword above his head in victory.

He shoved a hand through his hair as the ache of regret sank into him. She'd been furious, eyes flashing and voice cracking with rage.

She'd been distraught, her expressive eyes filled with disbelief—and tears.

And she'd been right.

He could have protected her from Textilecom by simply matching their stake. Even a well-placed phone call to the company could have put a stop to their buying. Not many executives relished the thought of going mano a mano with Declan Gates.

But no. Like a jealous lover he'd galloped in with his horses snorting, scattering other investors and seizing up huge chunks of stock. And he hadn't stopped until he'd strong-armed his way into a fifty-one-percent stake, thus ensuring no one—not even Lily—could own more of her company than he did.

He tugged at his tie, trying to loosen it further as his throat tightened. Had he thought she'd be thrilled?

No. He hadn't thought about her perspective at all. He'd tasted the thrill of victory, the bittersweet sting of triumph—just as he'd dreamed of doing when she first came to him with her plans to buy him out of Blackrock.

Ten long years and he'd almost succeeded in getting Lily Wharton out of his system. He'd made a life for himself, far from Maine. Charted a course that steered him to vast wealth and even a grudging measure of fame.

When he thought of his long-lost love it had been with a cool appraisal of his foolish younger self, if he even thought of her at all. He'd almost forgotten the sharp gaze of those hazel eyes and the arrogant tilt of her pretty chin.

Then she came roaring back in like a hot summer wind and blew him so far off course he'd probably never find his way back now.

He'd wanted revenge for the cold way she'd once discarded him. He'd lusted to seduce prim and perfect Lily Wharton and salivated at the prospect of seizing control of her company.

Then he got all tangled up in the silvery cord of memories and desire—and hope—that seemed to bind him to her whether he wanted it or not.

But when the chance to triumph came, he hadn't been able to stop himself. His killer instincts got the better of him. Now they were going to cost him the one woman he'd always wanted.

As he steered his bike to the exit of the parking garage, the attendant asked to see his pass. Declan flipped up the visor on his helmet and gave him a dark look.

The kid's eyebrows shot up. "Mr. Gates—that you?

I don't think I've ever seen anyone ride one of those in a suit before."

"First time for everything."

The attendant raised the barrier and Declan roared out into the street. Accusing fingers of light dipped between the tall buildings.

He gunned his engine and resolve surged inside him along with the roar of the motor.

First time for everything.

The wind slashed against his shirt and jacket, whipping them as he roared alongside the Hudson River. He rode aggressively, sliding from lane to lane and slipping in between cars as rush hour clogged the highways heading into New Jersey. He'd called Teterboro Airport and chartered a plane to Bangor.

He knew she'd go to Maine. That was her home base, her safe place, her harbor in the storm.

Even when the storm was *him*.

It was dark and misting with rain by the time he rode into Blackrock, near midnight. A chill wind bit at his skin as he rode along the cliff top over the silent town.

His house was dark, cold, empty, just as he'd intended it to remain forever.

Until Lily turned up.

He put the bike in the garage and headed for the front door. He couldn't resist looking out across the town to the cliff on the opposite side where the Wharton house sat, high as this one.

A thin yellow glow shone in an upper window.

That had always been Lily's room. His pulse kicked up and he cursed his instant reaction. How many nights had he stood here looking out at that lit window?

Lily must be there, right now.

A drop of rain trickled down his neck, in sharp contrast to the swell of heat stirring in his chest.

He had to see her.

Adrenaline pumped through his veins and kicked him back into action. He wheeled his bike out into the now-more-insistent rain and thick moonless dark, guiding the glinting key into the ignition by feel.

He couldn't sleep until he'd talked to her.

The sound of the engine fought the roar of rain as he rode—too fast—on the slick roads, turning his plan over in his mind.

Would she believe him? Would she forgive him?

Would she even see him?

He passed through the dark village, heading for the solitary house where that light still burned.

As he pulled onto a road leading up the cliff a slick patch of oil caused him to skid on the wet blacktop and slide at high speed toward the foot-high guardrail. As he steered the bike back into control in the nick of time, heart pounding, he realized he'd forgotten his helmet.

He'd bought one as soon as he dropped Lily off that day. She'd insisted that he get one and never ride without it.

She was the first person who'd ever said that to him.

As his rain-soaked hair stung his eyes, he realized that was another thing she was right about—and that he was screwing up right now.

* * *

Lily had calmed down considerably on the flight from Manhattan. Her mother had picked her up at the airport and she'd dampened her mom's CNBC-fueled enthusiasm by explaining Declan's actions in the simplest terms possible. Her mother had declared she'd expect nothing less from a Gates.

Lily didn't tell her mother she was pregnant with Declan's child. As they drove back from the station the secret hung in the air until it felt ready to burst out of her mouth, and she cursed herself for not spending the weekend at her apartment in Boston.

Once inside she excused herself and ran up to her room.

She lay on the bed and stared up at the ceiling, listening to the rain spatter against the window.

Her enthusiasm over her company's successful foray into the market was dampened—no, destroyed—by Declan's callous actions.

She had no idea if he planned a hostile takeover, or if his actions were just a power play to show her he could control her. Either way she didn't want to see him again as long as she lived.

A rumble outside sounded like thunder closing in from the ocean. The roar of it shivered through her and ripped loose a chunk of stray emotion.

Just when everything had been so perfect! Her company thriving, her plans to rebuild Blackrock swinging into action. Her long-lost love back in her arms and his baby growing inside her. Or so she'd dared to dream.

Regret and longing pinched her heart. What a fool she was.

A knock on the door startled her and she wiped a tear from her eye. "What? I'm sleeping," she lied.

"Declan Gates is at the door," her mother said, obviously irritated.

Panic shot through her, mingled with something else that she didn't want to examine. She did *not* want to see him. "Tell him to go away. It's after midnight."

"Delighted. What kind of barbarian would come knocking at this time?"

He'd come tonight? In the rain?

Something stirred in her heart.

Of course it would. She was a *sucker* for him.

She heard her mother's high-pitched voice at the foot of the stairs, but she couldn't make out the words over the patter of rain on the gabled roof. She listened as her mother slammed the door and walked back into the kitchen, muttering to herself.

The thunder had stopped. Or had it been Declan's bike? That sound always did make her shiver.

She listened for it to start up again. To take him away from her, as it had when he'd come to tell her he was leaving all those years ago.

Her ears strained but she couldn't hear anything except the incessant drizzle and the distant wash of waves on the beach.

A bang outside her window made her sit up in bed. A tree branch? No. There weren't any trees near the house.

She listened hard, sitting on the bed. Wrapped her

arms around herself. She had a strange sensation of being watched.

A loud rap on the window made her jump and shriek.

She turned and saw Declan's face hovering behind the window panes, lit only by the light from inside her room.

How on earth had he climbed up to the second-story window?

"Let me in."

She could barely make out his mouthed words through the glass. Rain smeared the image.

"No," she mouthed back. She should go close the curtains.

So why didn't she?

She heard a rattle and suddenly one side of the casement opened.

"These aren't very secure." He pushed it in, his soaked arm accompanied by a spray of rain. Her stomach jumped with fear or excitement or both.

"Go away." She managed to find the words.

"I don't think that's possible. At least not without a big jump." He winced. "I'm afraid I've accidentally detached your drainpipe from the wall."

Lily's eyes widened and she dashed to the window. Declan clung to the wood sill with both hands, his body braced against the rain-wet clapboard siding. He glanced at the empty space where the pipe usually rose to join the gutter above her window.

"What are you standing on?"

"I'm not." He shifted as he tried to get a better grip

on the window sill. "Save a life and let me in." She heard the effort in his voice as his eyes pleaded with her.

She fought a powerful urge to grab his arms and pull him in.

"Oh, come on, then." She walked away. He could go right through her bedroom and down the stairs. Her heart thudded so loud she was sure he could hear it.

He squeezed in through the narrow casement. His hair hung wet in his eyes and his white shirt was soaked through, revealing the absence of any kind of T-shirt underneath it. It clung to his skin and to the equally soaked black pants dripping copious amounts of rain-water onto her antique rag rug.

She could see the shadow of black hair that ran along the center of his torso. She could also see the swells of muscle that allowed him to scale her wall in the dead of night.

Treacherous heat curled in her belly.

"The door's that way," she managed, with a jerk of her head.

"I was wrong." His gray eyes blazed.

"Please leave my bedroom." Her voice sounded shrill.

"Listen to me. Just listen." He stepped toward her and she could smell the male scent of him, mingled with rain.

She held her chin high. "I don't want to hear another word from you, ever. Get out." She pointed at the door, her finger trembling.

"I'll give you back your shares." Raindrops glistened on his jaw. "I'll give you the factory and the house."

His words hung in the air.

Lily stared at him. Disbelief quickly turned to suspicion. "Do you really think I'd believe anything you say to me now? Look at you! You've invaded my room and now you're standing there dripping water and promises that have even less value. You wanted revenge on me and you got it. It's not my fault if it doesn't make you happy."

Declan pushed his wet hair off his face. "You're right, about everything. I did want revenge."

Lily stiffened. The lovemaking that she thought was so beautiful, so magical, had all been part of his cruel plan?

Her knees felt weak and she wondered if her heart could crumble into pieces.

He stared at her, eyes hooded, expression unreadable. "I could have sold to you right away. I could have offered you a fair price you could pay without taking your company public." He'd lowered his eyes while speaking, and now he glanced up at her through those thick lashes.

His pale eyes glittered with emotion. "That would have been the nice thing to do. Maybe even the right thing to do." He drew in a breath. "But I couldn't do it."

He stared straight at her, head cocked, gaze dark and piercing. "I wanted you to pay attention to me. I wanted you to *need* me."

Lily's heart squeezed. She'd hoped to buy the properties without even seeing him again.

That way she would have been safe.

She wrapped her arms around herself, hotly aware that Declan's baby was growing inside her, right now.

How would he react if he knew?

If he knew she—and their baby—needed him more than ever.

Tears pricked at her throat. "You achieved your goal." She tried to hold her voice steady. "I imagine there must be some satisfaction in that."

Declan looked at her. Storm clouds shadowed his eyes. "No." He shook his head. "I've realized that I've been wrong all along." His hand gesture scattered drops of water into the air, but he didn't seem to notice. "You told me to my face you regret how you treated me when we were kids. Even told me you started the rumor about me. You were brave enough to be honest." He hesitated and tension thickened the air. "I wasn't brave enough to be honest about my feelings."

She dug her fingernails into her palms. "That you wanted to hurt me."

"No." A cautious look shone in his eyes. "That I fell in love with you all over again."

His words sank in and a pang of stark emotion pierced her heart. "Then why?" she breathed.

"Because I didn't want to love you." His eyes narrowed. "I didn't want to give my heart to the woman who'd held it in her palm all those years ago, then threw it back at me when I least expected it. A man can't take that kind of hurt twice in a lifetime."

Lily's throat tightened. "I didn't want to hurt you again."

"No." He shook his head. "But you didn't want to need me, either. It took every ounce of self-control I had not to call you, to come see you. I wanted you to come to me for once, not because you needed to buy something from me, just because you wanted—*me*."

"I've been…" Thoughts of the baby and her hard-saved secret swam in her brain. "Busy. Very busy. You know how that goes." It wasn't a lie but the half-truth burned her tongue like acid.

"Yes. I do." He tilted his head and his eyes narrowed to dark slits. "I've kept busy ever since I left Blackrock years ago, kept my head down, buried in books, occupied with practicalities. Then you brought me back up here again and made me feel things I didn't want to feel."

His arms hung by his sides, his shirt cuffs dripping water onto the floor. "When you took your company public I wanted to support you. Buy a few shares to help boost your price." He pressed his lips together. "But when I noticed Textilecom gaining market share it triggered my competitive instincts."

He licked his lips. "Looking back I can see that I wanted to own your company. I wanted to own you. So you couldn't ignore me, you couldn't avoid me." His chest swelled beneath his wet shirt. "I did it because I love you." His eyes burned with emotion so raw she could almost sense it in the air.

Anger and shame fought in Lily's chest. She had avoided him. She'd deliberately put her feelings for him on hold—turned her attention to business. And in doing so she'd kept from him the news that he was going to be a father.

But perhaps she'd been right to be cautious if his

way of showing love was to make a power play to dominate her.

A sob ripped from her throat. "That's some way to show your love, Declan. Some people would send flowers."

"We're long past the flower stage, you and I, Lily." His steady gaze rocked her. "And I don't know how you truly feel about me, but I'm going to tell you how I feel about you."

He stared at her, his eyes soft. "I love you, Lily. Forget about what happened years ago, I love the person you are now. You're brave and fierce and beautiful and you don't let anything or anyone stand in your way."

Lily's eyes widened and a fire burned in her chest.

"Your plans for Blackrock prove that you combine deep caring with sharp practicality. The force of your vision and your energy is an inspiration. I thought I knew what I was doing, breaking down companies, building them up, swapping them around—all without any emotion involved, but your vision for this town has showed me what you can aim for if you put your heart in it, too."

Her breath came in shallow gulps.

"You *should* have the house and factory. There's no better person on this earth to take them into the future." He reached a hand into his back pocket. His wet shirt strained against hard muscle as he pulled something out and held it up in the light.

A folded envelope. Rather smudged.

"It's for you. A letter of promise transferring ownership of the properties and granting you a gift of the shares."

Lily bit her lip and stared at the rumpled, damp envelope. Her heart thudded.

"Take it." His eyes shone.

The emotion carried in his gesture stung her fingers as she took the soggy paper.

With shaking hands she opened the envelope and pulled out a single sheet. Printed in black and signed with a dark scrawl was the exact promise Declan had made.

"You mean it." Her voice came out breathless.

Guilt stabbed her heart. He'd put his heart on the table, along with millions of dollars worth of property and securities, and she still clung to the shocking secret that he was going to be a father.

Declan shoved a hand through his damp hair. "Today—yesterday by now—was a rude awakening for me. I don't want to spend the rest of my life engaged in a battle for some brass ring that I don't really care about. I have more money than I could ever need and I want to put it to work making the kinds of positive changes in the world that you plan to make in Blackrock. I've carried bitterness and resentment in my heart for too long. I don't want to bear that burden anymore."

The paper trembled in Lily's hand. She didn't deserve to hear Declan pour out his heart. But he didn't stop.

"I do love you, Lily." His voice was thick. "I'm telling you that straight out because from now on I plan to express myself in words and deeds instead of covert actions. I asked for your trust and you gave it to me. Then I betrayed it. I did it out of love but I know that's no excuse. I promise on everything I own and everything I am that I'll never do that again. Can you ever forgive me?"

The force of his emotion radiated from him, almost visible like steam in the muggy atmosphere of the room. Lily's own feelings grew and swirled around her as she struggled for words to respond.

She inhaled a shaky breath. "Yes, of course I can." Conviction roared through her, painful in its intensity. "I love you, too, Declan. I couldn't admit it even to myself. I guess I'm still afraid of my feelings, of not being in control. I didn't dare give you that kind of power over me. But by being secretive I only compounded the suspicion and fear and hurt that we couldn't seem to move past."

Her hands vibrated with the need to touch him. But not yet. "But I'll tell you the truth right now." She held her head high. "I've always loved you. I never stopped, not really. I think in a strange way I've been waiting for you all these years. Hoping and praying that one day you'd come back for me."

She hesitated and her fingers roamed unconsciously to her belly as it tightened with anticipation. She drew in a shaky breath. "I'm having our baby."

Declan's lips parted. He stared at her. Blinked. "What?"

Lily tucked a strand of hair behind her ear, suddenly nervous. "I'm pregnant."

He glanced at her belly. She grew self-conscious of her not-too-sexy cotton nightgown.

"You're pregnant, right now?" His words tumbled out as his eyes widened.

She nodded. "It must have happened the first time we…made love. On the beach." Her voice cracked.

His expression was blank, stunned. "You did say you love me, didn't you?"

His strange question confused her. "Yes." She searched his face and saw a mix of emotions wash over it.

"Can I…" He hesitated, and his brow furrowed. "Can I touch you, Lily? Can I hold you?"

His question was a plea. She could feel his desperation thick in the air and it echoed in her own lonely body.

They stepped forward and seized each other, holding so tight they could hardly breathe.

Declan's breath came in hard gasps, and her own emerged as sobs as she pressed her face into his neck and inhaled the reassuring male scent of him.

"God, I can't stand to be without you, Lily." His voice was gruff.

Lily rubbed her cheek against the wet collar of his shirt. "I've been longing to talk to you. But I didn't want to tell you about the pregnancy over the phone and I couldn't speak to you and not tell you." She turned her head to look up at him. "I had no idea how you'd react."

Declan pulled back a fraction, just until they could see each other's faces. His shone with raw joy that sparkled in his eyes. "Are you really having our baby, truly?"

She nodded, as tears pricked her eyes.

Declan's face grew serious. He loosened his arms from around her and drew back. He rubbed a hand over his mouth, thoughtful.

He glanced down at his disheveled wet clothes and

blew out a breath. "This isn't quite how I pictured this moment." She saw his Adam's apple move as he swallowed. He inhaled deeply and knelt down with one knee on the floor.

Lily's heart squeezed.

He picked up her left hand, which hung by her side.

"Lily. My lovely Lily. You're the only woman in the world I've ever loved. The only woman I will ever love." He hesitated. "Will you be my wife?" He looked up at her, his silver eyes shining with hope.

Tears fell as she managed to whisper the word *yes*.

Declan bent and kissed her ring finger. Her skin tingled as if a diamond sparkled on it.

His voice was gruff. "I don't have a ring, but I give you my heart to keep forever. Will that do for now?"

Lily couldn't help the half sob, half laugh that came along with, "Sure. But only if you kiss me right this instant."

He climbed to his feet and wrapped her in his arms. His mouth settled over hers, hot and urgent. Weeks of agonizing hope and fear fell away as she clutched him and pressed her fingertips into his wet shirt, into his firm muscle.

Their kiss was deep and fierce, filled with all the passion they'd stored and suppressed for so many years. Somewhere along the way she'd dropped the paper covered with his promises, but it didn't matter anymore.

She trusted him.

She slid her fingers underneath the wet cotton of his shirt and ran them over his hot skin, holding him close. "Do you think you could live in Blackrock again, Declan?"

She held her breath.

"I could live anywhere with you, Lily, but I want to live here, in the house. You've made it a home for the first time since I can remember. You've brought it back to life."

Lily pressed her cheek against his rough one, her heart so filled with hope it could burst. "I know the townspeople weren't kind to you, but I'm sure that once they get to know you… Get to know *us*…"

"And find out that rumor about me is actually true." His dark voice slid into her ear. "I seduced a local girl and got her pregnant."

A laugh shook them. "Well, there is that. Dangerous Declan rides again."

"Literally. I bet they're already cursing about my bike engine."

"Let them. This town is lucky to have you." She squeezed him, enjoying the warm moisture from his clothes as it seeped through her thin nightgown. "*I'm* lucky to have you. I was an idiot all those years ago, but I won't let other people make up my mind for me ever again. I love you, Declan Gates."

"And I love you, Lily Wharton."

His throaty voice curled into her ears and settled comfortably in her brain as they lost themselves in a soul-stirring kiss.

Epilogue

Chords from the ancient organ boomed through Blackrock's small chapel, filling the tall, narrow space with melodic sound.

The line of townspeople filed through the doorway, wreathed in smiles, murmuring compliments that filled Lily's heart.

"What a lovely baby. Just like a little angel."

"Thanks, Mrs. Winston." Lily stroked a silky black lock of her baby's hair back into place. Little James was uncharacteristically peaceful this morning. Maybe aware of how momentous an occasion his christening was for the town.

The symbolic union of the Gateses and the Whartons had begun with Declan and Lily's wedding last fall, and now it was personified in the most beautiful baby in the world.

And she could still say that after two weeks of being woken up at least five times a night.

"Isn't he sweet!" Mrs. Da Silva leaned over him. "Congratulations, Mrs. Gates."

Lily still hadn't got used to people calling her Mrs. Gates. Legally she'd kept both names, but apparently the people of Blackrock were too traditional for that. And it did feel good to share the same name with Declan.

She looked up at him standing beside her, shaking hands and exchanging pleasantries, a mile-wide grin spread across his handsome face.

"Excuse me for mentioning business, Lily." Flora Sampson, her production manager for the Blackrock mill, stepped up. "But we got the Anderson order finished last night." She beamed.

"Wow. Did you call in fairies to help?"

Flora's dangly earrings shook as she laughed. "No one would hear of going home until it was done. I think we all enjoy our weekends more if we're glowing with pride over another shipment of beautiful papers being created."

Lily smiled. She had the best workforce on the planet. "Make sure everyone gets double time for every second of overtime, okay?"

Declan couldn't believe how loyal and devoted Lily's employees were. They'd probably work for free if they could afford it. She treated them like much-loved family members. Which, in a way, they were, since Lily saw the whole town of Blackrock as her extended family.

And now he was part of that family, too.

"Can I hold him for a minute?" he whispered in Lily's ear. She gave him a conspiratorial smile. "Only if you kiss me first."

He obliged, unable to stop his eyes closing as their mouths met, even in front of all these people.

His lips tingled as he pulled back, and Lily settled little James in his arms.

"Goodness me, what a likeness!" A woman about Lily's mom's age touched the baby's cheek with her thumb. He curbed the urge to growl protectively. He was adjusting—slowly—to the fact that people didn't view him as the enemy of their peace and prosperity anymore.

Lily smiled. "He does look just like his dad, doesn't he?"

"It's too early to tell," he protested. "His eyes haven't changed color yet. Maybe they'll be hazel like his mom's." Whenever his son looked up at him he saw Lily's passion and devotion shining in that cherubic face.

And the kid had already demonstrated a good amount of determination to always be in someone's arms. Declan held his tiny body close. Who could blame him?

The woman looked from Lily to Declan. "You two do make a lovely couple."

Who'd have thought it?

The unspoken words hung in the air but Declan didn't mind. He and Lily had had a lot of fun going public with their relationship, enjoying the shock and disapproval that turned into amazement, then wonder, then—and he honestly believed it—joy.

People really were happy to see the rift between the two families healed. It signaled a new chapter in the history of Blackrock and in the lives of everyone in the town.

Lily's business involved almost every single townsperson one way or another. She even had a lot of the garrulous older ladies driving around local towns, hawking her samples to local merchants and renovators, to make sure the business was truly local, as well as national.

The vicar swept up behind Declan and Lily and put his arm around them both. "The little tyke ready to get wet?"

"I think he'll let us know how he feels at the top of his lungs." Lily's smile didn't hide her nerves.

"I'll hold him," said Declan. He linked his arm with Lily's so no one could tug either of them away from him. This kid wasn't going to experience any lack of affection or attention, nor was his wife.

Emotion made his chest feel tight. "I'll let him know it's just a new experience." He wanted his son to have the best of everything—not in the way the old Whartons and Gateses thought of it, as a bunch of possessions or power to wield over people—but the best of everything he and Lily had shared when they were kids. The beauty of the countryside, the power of the ocean, the magic in the air that made anything possible in their own little paradise on a cliff on the edge of the world.

* * * * *

Silhouette®

Desire

NEW YORK TIMES BESTSELLING AUTHOR

DIANA PALMER

A brand-new Long, Tall Texans novel

IRON COWBOY

Available March 2008 wherever you buy books.

Visit Silhouette Books at www.eHarlequin.com SD76856IBC

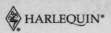

HARLEQUIN®

INTRIGUE

BREATHTAKING ROMANTIC SUSPENSE

Look for

UNDER
HIS SKIN

BY RITA HERRON

Nurse Grace Gardener brought
Detective Parker Kilpatrick back from
the brink of death, only to seek his
protection. On a collision course with
two killers who want to keep their
secrets, she's recruited the one detective
with the brass to stop them.

Available February wherever you buy books.

BECAUSE THE BEST PART
OF A GREAT ROMANCE
IS THE MYSTERY.

REQUEST YOUR FREE BOOKS!

2 FREE NOVELS PLUS 2 FREE GIFTS!

Silhouette® *Desire*®

Passionate, Powerful, Provocative!

$1.00 OFF

The bestselling Lakeshore Chronicles continue with *Snowfall at Willow Lake*, a story of what comes after a woman survives an unspeakable horror and finds her way home, to healing and redemption and a new chance at happiness.

SUSAN WIGGS

On sale February 2008!

SAVE $1.00

off the purchase price of **SNOWFALL AT WILLOW LAKE** by Susan Wiggs.

Offer valid from February 1, 2008, to April 30, 2008.
Redeemable at participating retail outlets. Limit one coupon per purchase.

52608168

5 65373 00076 2   (8100) 0 11463

MSW2493CPN

Texas Hold 'Em

When it comes to love, the stakes are high

Sixteen years ago, Luke Chisum dated
Becky Parker on a dare…before going
on to break her heart. Now the former
River Bluff daredevil is back, rekindling
desire and tempting Becky to pick up
where they left off. But this time she has
to resist or Luke could discover the secret
she's kept locked away all these years.…

Look for

TEXAS BLUFF

by Linda Warren

#1470

Available February 2008
wherever you buy books.

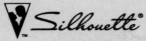

Romantic
SUSPENSE

Sparked by Danger, Fueled by Passion.

When Tech Sergeant Jacob "Mako" Stone opens
his door to a mysterious woman without a past,
he knows his time off is over. As threats to Dee's
life bring her and Jacob together, she must set
aside her pride and accept the help of the military
hero with too many secrets of his own.

Out of Uniform
by Catherine Mann

Available February wherever you buy books.

You can lead a horse to water…

When Alyssa Barkley and Clint Westmoreland
found out that their "fake" marriage was never
rendered void, they are forced to live together
for thirty days. However, Clint loves the single
life and has no intention of being tamed, but
when Alyssa moves in, the sizzling attraction
between them is ignited and neither wants the
thirty days to end.

Look for

TAMING CLINT WESTMORELAND

by

BRENDA JACKSON

Available February wherever you buy books

COMING NEXT MONTH

#1849 PRIDE & A PREGNANCY SECRET—
Tessa Radley
Diamonds Down Under
She wants to be more than his secret mistress, especially now that she's pregnant with his heir. But she isn't the only one with a secret that could shatter a legacy.

#1850 TAMING CLINT WESTMORELAND—
Brenda Jackson
They thought their fake marriage was over...until they discovered they were still legally bound—with their attraction as strong as ever.

#1851 THE WEALTHY FRENCHMAN'S PROPOSITION—
Katherine Garbera
Sons of Privilege
Sleeping with her billionaire boss was not on her agenda. But discovering they were suddenly engaged was an even bigger surprise!

#1852 DANTE'S BLACKMAILED BRIDE—Day Leclaire
The Dante Legacy
He had to have her. And once he discovered her secret, he had the perfect opportunity to blackmail his business rival's daughter into becoming his bride.

#1853 BEAUTY AND THE BILLIONAIRE—
Barbara Dunlop
A business mogul must help his newest employee transform from plain Jane to Cinderella princess...but can he keep his hands off her once his job's done?

#1854 TYCOON'S VALENTINE VENDETTA—
Yvonne Lindsay
Rekindling a forbidden romance with the daughter of his sworn enemy was the perfect way to get his revenge. Then he discovers she's pregnant with his child!

SDCNM0108